MW01331793

# The Smiling One-eyed Creatures

The Smiling One-eyed Creatures

© Copyright 2024 by Tim Callahan.  All rights reserved.

No part of this publication may be reproduced, stored in a retrieval system or transmitted in any way by any means, electronic, mechanical, photocopy, recording or otherwise without the prior permission of the author except as provided by USA copyright law.
This novel is a work of fiction.

Cover design by Jim Culler & Cārucandra Klupp
Cover Photography by Jim Culler
**ISBN:** 9798335100205
Published in the United States of America by Kindle Direct
1. Fiction / Young Adult, Adult

# The Smiling One-eyed Creatures

By

Tim Callahan

# *Books by*

# *Tim Callahan*

Kentucky Summers Series 1:

1. The Cave, the Cabin & the Tattoo Man
2. Coty & the Wolf Pack
3. Dark Days in Morgan County
4. Above Devil's Creek
5. Timmy & Susie & the Bootleggers' Revenge
6. Kentucky Snow & the Crow
7. Red River, Junior & the Witch
8. Forever the Pack

Kentucky Summers Series 2:

1. Muddied Waters
2. We Saw Something
3. The Indian Summer of '64
4. The Sound of Tears
5. Treehawk
6. Roadkill in Blaze
7. Tick
8. A Broken Wing
9. Purty & the Chicken Thieves
10. Skirter & the Secret Barn
11. Bigfoot Bedlam & the Snake

Children's Illustrated Book

Timmy & Susie - Catching Crawdads

Other stand-alone novels:

Sleepy Valley
Come Home, Joe
Nashville Sounds
Leah's Path
The Smiling One-eyed Creatures

*This book is dedicated*

**To:**

*My good friend,*

*Terry Cornett*

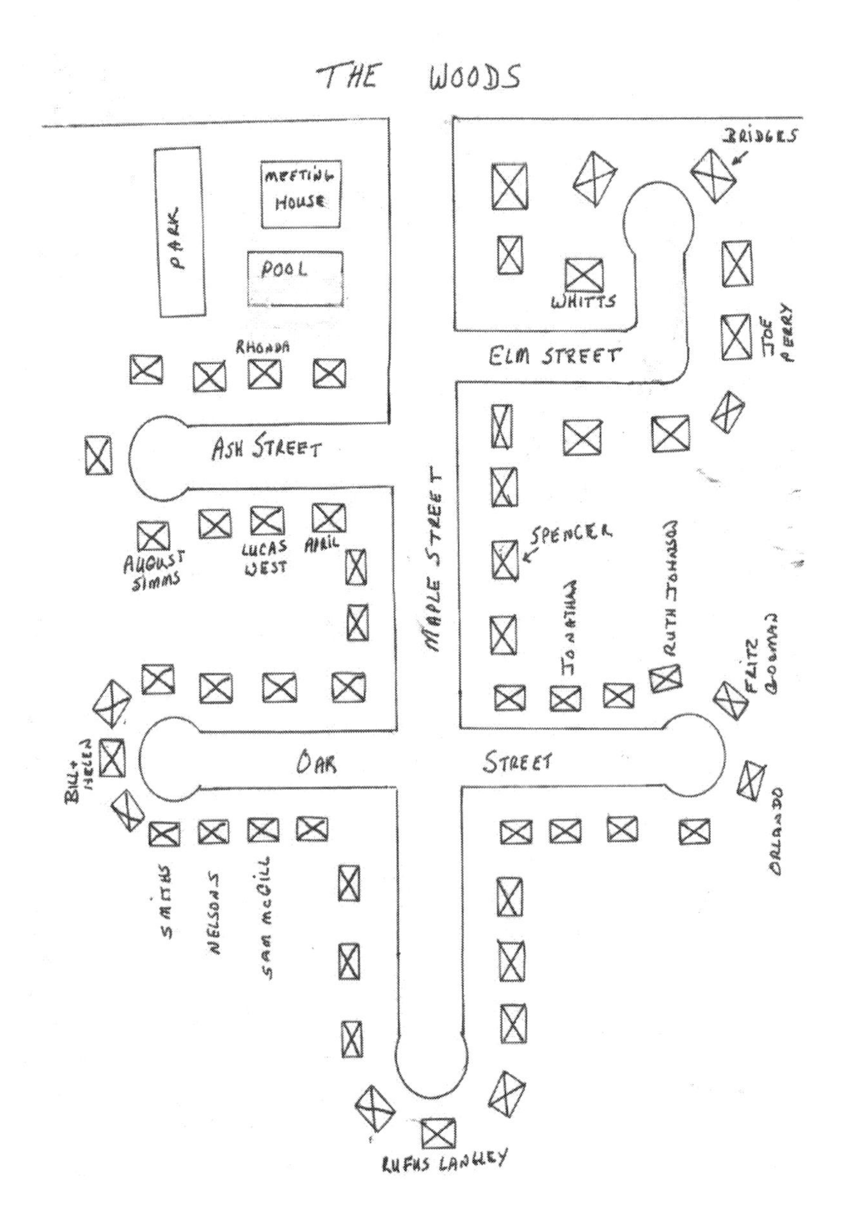
THE WOODS
BRIDGES
MEETING HOUSE
PARK
POOL
WHITTS
JOE PERRY
ELM STREET
RHONDA
ASH STREET
MAPLE STREET
SPENCER
RUTH JOHNSON
JONATHAN
AUGUST SIMMS
LUCAS WEST
APRIL
FRITZ GOODMAN
BILL + HELEN
OAK
STREET
ORLANDO
SMITHS
NELSONS
SAM McGILL
RUFUS LANGLEY

# URP

***Meaning-*** *Urp is slang for vomiting or throwing up, used to express disgust or being grossed out by something.*

## Chapter 1

Saturday in June, Minnesota

***It was a sunny Saturday in June*** in the quiet Minnesota neighborhood, seventy-two degrees, not a cloud in the sky. On Oak Street, Sam McGill went out to his neat, well-kept shed and hopped on his riding mower. His wife had promised their neighbors, Tom and Shiela Nelson, that Sam would mow their yard while they were away to Cancun on a vacation. He noticed that the neighbors on the other side of the Nelsons were having some sort of party, a cookout it looked like.

Sam knew he would be disturbing their party, but the Nelsons were due back the next day and he had neglected to mow the yard all week. He decided he could quickly mow the back yard in ten minutes and be done. Besides, with his headphones on, it wouldn't be that disturbing.

He had not yet met the new couple who were hosting the party. They had just moved in a couple of months earlier.

It would have been nice if they had invited him and his wife, Patsy, not that he would have attended. He thought it was rude of them. He decided he really didn't care if he disturbed their outdoor party.

He began mowing up against the back of the house. He noticed rows of flowers extending from the house. How in the world was he going to be able to mow between them on his riding mower? He looked up to see the guests of the party watching him. While looking at them, he ran over a few of the flowers. Oh well, they had plenty. He wasn't getting paid for mowing their yard, he was doing it out of the kindness of his heart. What do a few flowers matter?

He mowed on around the rows and closer to the party when the new neighbor motioned him over. He rode the mower to where they stood. He took his headphones off and stopped the mower.

"Hi. You live on the other side of the Nelsons, don't you?"

"Yeah." He figured the next question would be if he minded not mowing while their party was going on. He was wrong.

"I'm John Smith." He extended his hand. "George and Mitchell," he said, introducing the two men with him.

Sam shook his hand and said, "Sam McGill." Sam figured the guy was playing nice before asking him to stop mowing.

"Sam, we found this in our yard. Never seen anything like it. You know what it is?"

He handed Sam the almond shaped object that looked to be some kind of nut. It was maybe two inches wide and an inch or so high. The rough looking shell resembled an old walnut, creased and wrinkled. But it was more of an oval shape.

Sam held it in his hand and inspected it. He had never seen anything like it, and thinking he was pretty much an expert in everything, he said, "Looks like some kind of nut."

"Like maybe a chestnut or hickory nut?"

"They're smaller than this. There are a lot of different nuts in this area," Sam said, not really knowing if his statement was true or not.

Mitchell said, "But there's not a nut tree anywhere within sight of where we found it."

"A squirrel must have brought it from the woods and dropped it. Stupid pests like to bury nuts for the winter," Sam explained. While he was explaining, he was also digging with his fingernail at the exterior of the nut-like object. He dug his fingernail into a crevice and pried it up until a piece of the shell broke off.

He closely looked inside. It was dark inside. He squinted to see a face looking back at him. "What in the name of God is that?" he said as he extended his arm as far as it would reach, not wanting the thing close to his face. The three other men came closer and peered into the shell that Sam held. The wormlike object bared its human-like teeth and opened its yellow, cat-like eye that erupted out of its face toward them.

The three men screamed. It couldn't have been more than an inch long but was as scary as heck.

"What the Hell?!"

"It's demonic!"

"Kill that thing!" they yelled.

Sam brought it closer to his face for inspection. The worm's body was almost a transparent yellow color, but its face was dark except for its teeth and eye. It had tiny ears sticking up from the top of its head.

"Beats all I've ever seen," Sam said as he watched the thing double in size to where the head was now sticking out of the shell. The wives of the three men hurried over when they heard the screams. When they saw the small beast turn its head toward them and grin, they screamed louder than their husbands and backed away.

"What is that?!" one of them yelled.

"Drop it on the ground and stomp on it!" John yelled.

Sam dropped it to the ground. Everyone looked down at it.

"Somebody, stomp on it!" John yelled.

One of the men said, "I'm not getting that thing on the bottom of my shoe. You're the host! It's your yard. You stomp it!"

Sam saved the men the embarrassment when he said, "I'll run over it with the tire of the mower."

"Good idea!" John said. He was not going to stomp it.

Sam quickly got on the mower and started it. He even started the blades and lowered them to the lowest setting in case the thing came out of the shell. He would scalp the grass, but who cared as long as he killed the thing. He started toward it as the partygoers watched with great interest. Sam aimed carefully at the object and moved forward. He ran smack dab over it. He thought he even heard the shell crack over the sound of the mower.

"Well done!" the men shouted. As the men celebrated the death of the thing, Sam thought he caught something from the corner of his eye. He looked toward the edge of the house. He saw something that was more than ten times the size of the worm crawling in the grass around the corner of the house. But he figured it must have been something else, maybe a snake. It was way too big to have come out of the shell.

As the men and women were thanking Sam for a job well done, he decided to put off the mowing until their party was over, truthfully, he was too shaken to continue mowing. Even if it meant getting up early on a Sunday morning and mowing before his neighbors returned home. He never had anything to do on Sunday mornings anyway. They didn't attend church. He was a devout atheist. His wife never thought about it one way or the other.

*As Sam was putting his mower back* in the shed, three young boys were riding their bikes down the quiet street when a four-foot-long caterpillar looking thing came out from between two houses.

"What is that?!" Orlando screamed. The four foot long, burnt orange thing began chasing them down the street. The three boys wasted no time pedaling their bikes as fast as they could toward

Orlando's house. The thing was gaining on them. Its eye was extending further from its head. Tiny arms came out from the bottom of its body like a T-Rex.

"Faster!" the boy in the front screamed. Their feet were moving faster than they ever had. The lead boy, Orlando, made a slight turn into his driveway and straight into the open garage. He skidded to a quick stop. The other two bicyclists were somewhere behind him.

Olando dropped his bike on the garage cement and ran to hit the garage door opener. The other two boys had ridden their bikes into the garage and dropped them. They watched as the thing turned into the driveway and raced toward the closing door.

"Hurry! Hurry!" Jonathan said.

Orlando screamed, "I can't make it go down any faster."

"It's going to come in after us!" Spencer screamed.

All three boys bent down to watch the monster, nervously hoping it would get shut out. Just as the door was six inches from the floor, the thing's eyeball whipped under the door, tripping the door's electric eye, and stared at them. The boys screamed. The door started to go back up. Orlando hit the button again and the door started back down. The eyeball then slipped back under the door allowing it to fully close.

"What the heck was that?!" Spencer said.

"A giant caterpillar?" Orlando offered.

"That was no caterpillar. I think it was a nightmare," Jonathan said.

Spencer said, "Maybe we're all in a nightmare. Somebody pinch me."

Orlando reached over and pinched his side.

"Hey. That hurt. I wasn't serious."

"You aren't dreaming," Jonathan said.

"Maybe the pinch was in my dream," Spencer said. "What else could explain that creature?"

"Is it gone?" Jonathan asked.

"How would we know? There're no windows in here," Orlando answered. "Living room!"

The boys ran into the house toward the nearest window.

They hurried to the front bay window to look for the thing. Orlando pulled the curtains open, and they pressed their faces against the glass looking out into the yard and street. It was nowhere to be seen.

"I'm never going outside again," Spencer said.

"How are you getting home?" Jonathan asked.

"I live here now," Spencer answered.

"Mom doesn't like you that much," Orlando told him.

"That's hurtful," Spencer faked tears.

As they looked out at the street, the creature popped up from under the windowsill and wickedly grinned as its arms reached toward the glass, as though trying to grab them. They screamed so loud the next town may have heard them.

The caterpillar, wormlike thing crawled up the window looking for a way to get in. Its many legs had sucker feet that stuck to the window as it went along, leaving a sticky substance with each step.

"It can climb walls and windows," Orlando said.

"Does it look longer than it did before?" Jonathan asked.

"I didn't stop long enough to measure it," Orlando said.

"It does look longer" Spencer agreed.

The thing stretched across the entire six-foot bay window.

"Where is it going?" Jonathan asked.

Orlando again stuck his head inside the bay window to look for the beast.

"It's heading up toward the roof," he told his two eighth-grade classmates.

"It could come down the chimney!" Spencer cried out.

"Would it fit?" Jonathan asked.

"It's not as fat as Santa Claus," Spencer said. The other two boys just looked at him wondering if he was serious.

It looked to be around a two-foot diameter, but they didn't know it had the ability to also shrink down in size to get into small places.

"Quick! We need to block the fireplace so it can't get in the house!"

"With what?" Jonathan asked.

"Pillows," Spencer suggested.

The boys began taking the cushions and pillows off the couch and chairs in the living room. Orlando stuffed them into the opening as the other two boys brought them to him.

"He could push through those. Let's put something in front of the fireplace to block them," Orlando told them.

"What?"

Orlando looked around the room for something they could use. "The recliner," he finally said.

They went over to the recliner and struggled to move it across the room to place it securely against the cushion-stuffed fireplace. They had covered the opening.

"That should do it," Orlando said as they stood back and looked at their work.

"What do we do now?" Spencer asked.

Orlando thought about it and then said, "Internet. There's got to be something about this thing on the internet. I'll be back." He ran to get his laptop.

# Chapter 2

***Meanwhile***, Sam McGill had entered his house and taken a seat in his favorite recliner. His wife, Patsy, walked into the room on her way to their bedroom. She looked down at her husband and saw the worried look on his face.

"What's wrong, Sam?"

"Oh. Nothing." Sam wouldn't say what he saw. He didn't want his wife to think he was going crazy.

***Orlando turned his laptop*** on and was ready to type in something. But he hesitated, he had no idea what to type. He thought – Giant yellow caterpillar with a face and bulging eye, or – Creepy monster that looks like a huge walking banana with a bulging eye and T-Rex arms?

He closed the laptop. He realized there would be no help on the computer.

Spencer yelled out, "Your Mom is pulling in the driveway!"

"She'll open the garage door to park the car!" Orlando called out.

"Our bikes!" he yelled out.

They had dumped their bikes in the middle of the garage as they had escaped the monster. He heard the garage door opening as they ran through the house to put their bikes back up on their stands on the right side of the garage. His mother liked to park on the left side.

She watched them as she waited for the boys to move the bikes. They watched the opening for the creature. She had told her son a hundred times where to put his bike. As soon as her car was inside, Sam pushed the button to close the large garage door and then watched to see if the creature would slide into the garage and attack his mother. Finally, the door closed against the cement floor.

"Hi, Mom."

"Hi, Honey. Why did you close the garage door? That makes it harder to get the groceries out." His Mom opened the trunk and pulled out a bag of groceries.

"We'll get those," Orlando said.

"That would be great. I've had quite a day," she said. It might get worse, Orlando thought.

"I got some snacks for you guys."

"Great," they all said.

She kissed the top of Orlando's head as she walked into the house. The three guys went to the trunk and removed the bags of groceries and put them on the kitchen counter.

Spencer grabbed a bag of Oreos and Jonathan took a shiny red apple. Once they were done, they walked back into the living room to find Orlando's mother standing in the center of the room staring at the cushion-barren furniture and the strangely situated recliner.

Without turning toward the boys she asked, "You mind explaining what happened here?"

"We needed to keep a monster out of the house, Mom," Orlando blurted out.

Not fazed, she said, "Whatever you're playing, there is no way you should be using my cushions and pillows. Put everything back the way they were. And before you put the cushions back on the couch take them outside and shake them off. They probably have soot all over them. You guys should have known better."

Orlando wasn't sure if he should continue trying to tell his mom about the monster or not. He knew it would be hard for her to believe. He had trouble believing it himself.

"After you get done with that. Take a pint of cream over to the McGill house. I borrowed some cream from Patsy earlier this week."

"I'm sure they don't expect you to give them back the cream," Orlando said. He did not want to go back outside knowing what was out there.

"It's the right thing to do," she said. "I'm going up to take a shower. It's been a long day. And please put the groceries away."

"I'm not going out there," Spencer said as soon as Mrs. Gomez went to her bedroom.

Orlando's parents had divorced when he was four, and his dad now lived in another state with his new family and saw Orlando seldom. His mother worked hard to keep the house. She was a cashier at the local grocery, and she worked part time cleaning houses. With the check from Orlando's dad each month she had managed to get by, but it was getting harder with the rising cost of everything.

Orlando was fourteen and left alone often. His mother was often gone for long stretches having two jobs to make ends meet. There had never been a problem leaving him home during the day while she was gone. He was very responsible for his age. He spent most of the time with his two best friends playing in the neighborhood.

The boys carried the recliner back to its spot and started putting the pillows and cushions back on the couch. They inspected each one to see if they needed to be taken outside and have the soot knocked off. Orlando would open the front door and take two steps onto the walk and beat it a few times before hurrying back inside the house, keeping an eye out for the thing.

The boys didn't know the monster had gone to the woods to hide.

Once the cushions were back on the couch, Spencer said, "I really think I might have to live here now. I'm never going back outside again." He was keeping an eye on the fireplace to make sure the creature didn't squeeze into the room.

"Let's take the cream to the McGills' house," Orlando said.

"I'm not going. What did I just say?" Spencer told him.

Orlando looked at Jonathan. Jonathan rolled his eyes and said, "Okay. But we have to ride our bikes."

"Okay." Orlando found the cream in one of the bags and put the rest of the refrigerated stuff into the fridge. The rest could wait until he returned, if he ever returned, he thought.

Orlando told Spencer, "Close the garage door when we leave."

Spencer was carrying around the poker from the fireplace.

The two boys opened the garage door and jumped onto their bikes. They carefully peeked around the corners before exiting, and then sped down the driveway and onto the street. He heard the garage closing. Sam McGill's' house was only eight houses away, but on that day, it seemed like a mile. They kept looking over their shoulders as they pedaled down the street.

Orlando rang the doorbell to Sam McGill's house. Sam was still sitting in his recliner recovering from his encounter. When he heard the doorbell he shouted, "Patsy! The door! You need to get the door!"

When there was no response, he huffed. The bell rang again. He got up and walked to the door. He opened it a bit and looked out. He saw the two boys standing on his stoop. He had seen them many times, but didn't remember their names nor did he care.

"You only need to ring once. Patience, learn patience. There's only so many rings in a doorbell."

"How many?" Jonathan asked.

Orlando said, "My mother sent this to replace the cream she borrowed."

Sam opened the door all the way, figuring the creature, if it was still alive, would get the boys before it got to him.

"Your mother borrowed cream?"

"I guess so. Here it is." Orlando handed the cream to Sam.

"Can I ask you a question?" Orlando then asked. Before waiting for him to answer he asked, "Have you seen anything strange in the neighborhood today?"

Sam looked at the boy. He could tell that the boy had seen the wormlike creature also.

"What are you talking about?"

"Oh, a creature about six feet long with a bulging eye and lots of legs," Orlando said.

"And arms like a T-Rex. And it can climb buildings with its sucker feet," Jonathan added.

"I've seen nothing of the sort. Thanks for the cream," he said.

He closed the door on the boys and wondered what in the world was happening.

The two boys stood there looking at the door that was slammed in their faces.

"Nice guy," Jonathan said, sarcastically.

"I think he knows something. Did you see the look on his face when we mentioned the creature?"

"I don't know. He always has a scowl on his face. He reminds me of Scrooge," Jonathan said.

The boys turned and went back to their bikes and took off riding as fast as they could back to Orlando's house. They dumped their bikes in the front yard and ran to the door. Spencer opened it and hurried them inside.

"Did you see it?" Spencer asked.

"No. But we saw another monster," Jonathan said.

"What?"

"He's talking about Mr. McGill," Orlando said.

"He's a mean old guy. One day, I heard him cuss out a rabbit that was crossing his front yard," Spencer said. Spencer stuck another cookie in his mouth. He had chocolate from the Oreos stuck between his teeth.

Orlando went to the kitchen and started putting away the other groceries. Jonathan helped him. Spencer was keeping watch at the front window.

"It could be in the back yard, Spence!" Jonathan yelled out. Orlando looked out the window that was above the sink but didn't see anything. Spencer came running through the house to the eating area window.

"I don't see anything," Spencer told them.

"What could be in the backyard?" Orlando's mom asked.

Her hair was still damp from the shower, and she was wearing casual shorts and a tee shirt. She was a good-looking woman. Spencer was always telling Orlando how cute his mother was. Orlando thought it was a creepy thing to say.

"You look nice, Mrs. Gomez," Spencer said.

"Don't change the subject. What could be in the backyard?" she asked again.

"I saw a hawk fly over the house, and it looked like it might land back there," Orlando said. He never lied to his mother. But he didn't feel like he should tell her the truth.

"What would you like for supper?" she asked. "Would you boys like to stay?"

"Sure. Could I spend the night?" Spencer asked.

"Spaghetti," Orlando said.

"That sounds easy enough. Of course, you can spend the night as long as I talk to your parents," she told Spencer.

"You might as well stay also," Orlando said to Jonathan.

"Okay."

"The truth was that neither of the boys were anxious to go outside to their homes. Spending the night where they were safe sounded great."

"Put some water on to boil. I'll put some Texas toast in the oven," Orlando's mom told him.

Spencer kept an eye out for the creature in the backyard.

"I'll call my mom," Jonathan said. His dad was away on a business trip and his mother was home with his two younger siblings. A sister who was ten and a brother who was six. His mother had never worked, although she volunteered one day a week at the animal shelter.

After asking his mom about spending the night he handed the phone to Mrs. Gomez. It was fine for him to spend the night.

Spencer then tore himself away from the window to call home. His parents were more than happy to let Spencer spend the night at Orlando's house. His parents had been going through a rough spell and lately had done nothing but argue. He thought they might be divorcing. They both worked long hours and seldom spent much time together. He figured with him being away it would give them more opportunity to fight. He was an only child, like Orlando.

**Rufus Langley** was taking his evening hike through the woods behind his house. He lived at the end of Maple Street. There were trails throughout the forest that the residents often walked and where their children often played. They were perfectly safe. A couple of treehouses had been built and forts constructed among the trees.

As Rufus walked at a steady pace, he noticed something on the ground near the path. At first, he thought they were walnuts, upon picking one up and inspecting it, he knew they weren't. They were odd shaped, oblong and winkled looking. He found three of them on the ground.

He looked up into the trees to see if he could find where they could have fallen from. None of the trees held whatever these things were. He put them in his pocket and continued his hike. He carried them home with him.

*Orlando's home* was at the end of Oak Street on the cul-de-sac. If a driver was coming down Oak Street and went straight, instead of going around the circle, he would just miss hitting their house. Behind their backyard were woods where the boys often played and explored. They had built a fort and added to it over the years to where it was beginning to look more like a house. As houses were being built in the neighborhood, the boys would ask the builders for the scrap wood. They were happy to get rid of it, especially when they found out what it was going to be used for.

Every man, that had once been a boy, had wanted to build a fort or a treehouse to escape to. There was a community park on the right as you entered The Woods. The swimming pool and meeting house were positioned in front of the park. It had the usual slides and swings and climbing apparatuses. It also had a nice picnic area with tables and grills. Orlando always wondered why a family would want to pack up and have a cookout at the park instead of doing it in their own backyard. It made no sense to him.

*Pretty African American,* August Simms, lived on Ash Street. She was going into the eighth grade with Orlando, whom she had a deep crush on. She had liked him since the fourth grade. He was nice to her and talked to her, but nothing more. She wanted him to be her boyfriend. He acted as though he had no interest in having her, or anyone else for that matter, as his girlfriend.

After eating supper with his mom and two friends, Orlando was standing at the front bay window looking outside for the creature when he saw August riding her bicycle toward his house. He would see her riding past almost every day. He figured she must have a usual routine that she took.

He opened the front door and ran out, closing the door behind him. He heard Spencer yell, "What are you doing!?"

He ran down to the street to intercept August. He looked around making sure the creature wasn't around.

August stopped and got off her seat and stood straddling the bike. "Hi, Orlando." Her big smile was due to him coming out to see her.

"Hi, August. You need to go home and stay in your house."

Her smile disappeared. "What?"

"It's hard to explain. But there's a monster on the loose."

She looked hard at him and said, "If you want to get rid of me you could just say that. What an awful thing to say!"

"August, I don't want to get rid of you. I'm telling you the truth. Spencer, Jonathan and I were chased by it earlier. It's awful! You need to get home as quickly as you can. I'm trying to protect you."

"It's too bad it didn't catch you!" she angrily said aa she got back on her seat and took off. "I've been nothing but nice to you!" she yelled.

"I'm telling you the truth!" he yelled as she rode away.

Spencer and Jonathan were watching from the window.

"He's risking his life for a girl," Jonathan told Spencer.

"I'd risk my life for August," Spencer said.

"You'd risk your life for any girl, even Penelope Peters," Jonathan told him. Penelope was the weirdest girl in their class. She was a thin, wiry specimen of a girl who was always wiping her nose with her sleeve. She sounded like a mouse when she talked and wore nothing but green clothing.

"No way. Not Penelope," Spencer said.

Orlando ran back into the house, locking the door behind him.

"Why did you do that?" Spencer asked.

"I had to warn her."

"Did she believe you?" Jonathan asked.

"No. She thought I was just trying to get rid of her. Why would I care if she rode her bike on my street? She does it all the time."

"That's because she likes you, stupid," Spencer said.

"She does not. She just yelled at me."

"That's because you told her to go home, idiot."

"She doesn't like me like that," Orlando said, starting to doubt himself.

"She's liked you for years," Spencer said.

# Chapter 3

*Coming* home after a long day at the pharmacy, Mr. Fritz Gorman, Orlando's neighbor on the cul-de-sac, saw something lying in the grass between the houses as he pulled into his driveway. He parked his car and got out. He walked over to what he now recognized as a dead squirrel. He went into the garage and retrieved a plastic bag and went back out to pick up the dead animal. When he bent over, he noticed that its belly had been ripped open.

This was strange, he thought. He picked it up and looked closer. He then noticed that the squirrel's liver had been removed. All the other organs seemed to be intact. He closed the bag around it and took it to the garbage can. He wondered what would have done such a thing to the squirrel.

Mr. Gorman and his wife, Jane, had only moved into the neighborhood four months earlier. Orlando thought they seemed nice but hadn't really gotten to know them very well.

He knew the neighbors on the other side of them. Sid and Nancy Coleman had lived there as long as they had. They had three kids. Two twin six-year-old girls and a three-year-old boy. Orlando was always doing favors for them. He was happy to do help them.

"I found the strangest thing outside," Fritz told his wife, Cathy.

"What was that, Dear?"

"A dead squirrel with its liver missing."

"What? Where did you find that?"

"In the grass between our house and the Gomez's house."

"Why would something do that?" Cathy asked. "You don't think those boys would have done that to a squirrel, do you?"

"No. I don't think they would do it. I figured it was another animal or bird, maybe. Perhaps a hawk. I've seen a few around. Probably because of the woods behind us."

**As darkness closed** in around the neighborhood the creature came out of the woods and crept around the backyards looking for more liver to eat. Squirrel liver, rabbit liver, human liver, it didn't matter, it wanted more liver.

Its maximum length was seven feet unless it needed to squeeze into a spot. It then could double its length and squeeze into a six-inch hole.

Earlier in the day it had deposited urps in the woods. Urps were egg like nuggets that held their offspring. They were oblong objects that looked like a walnut with its outside shell missing. When they were ready, they would break out. They would then grow to adult size very quickly and then be able to shrink and expand at will. They then needed to find liver to survive.

They varied in adult size. The biggest up to seven feet long with sixteen suctioned feet, two pointed ears, two small arms that came out from under its skin, and an eye that telescoped out to three feet or more.

The creature fertilized itself, thus not needing a mate to produce offspring. This process is called parthenogenesis and is found in other species. Normally it only hunted after dark, it only chased the boys in the daylight because that was when it was released from its shell.

It went into the backyards and between houses looking for prey. Mrs. Johnson's cat was let out of the back door just as it came around the corner of the house. The cat never stood a chance as the creature pounced on the cat and removed its liver, leaving the cat lying on the patio.

*The three boys* grew more tired with each passing moment. Orlando's mom had put on a scary movie for the boys to watch. She knew they always enjoyed horror films. But not tonight. Orlando looked over and said, "I think I'm going to bed."

"Me too," Spencer chimed in. Jonathan got up and followed.

"Goodnight, boys."

Once the boys had closed the bedroom door, Spencer said, "Why would you let her put on Nightmare on Elm Street? Aren't we scared enough already?"

Orlando had bunk beds. He took the bottom bunk while Spencer claimed the top. Orlando's mom had bought an easy electric blow-up mattress for when the two boys stayed over. Jonathan took the blow up.

"Why do I get the blow-up mattress?"

Spencer answered, "You're used to things that are inflatable. Like your girlfriend."

"Whoa!" Orlando said as he laughed. "You have a blow-up girlfriend?"

"No. You can't believe anything Spence says," Jonathan told him. "Spencer, you jerk!"

*Orlando's mom* checked the locks on the doors and turned off the lights before heading to her bedroom. She was tired also and had been falling asleep during the movie. She had never liked scary movies. Rom coms were her favorites. She quickly slipped into bed.

*Rufus Langley* had placed the odd nut-like things on his worktable in the basement. He was going to go back down and crack them open later that evening but got busy and forgot about them. The objects wiggled and moved as they lay on the table. They were ready to come out.

*The creature* moved around the houses, staying out of sight. It found the house where he had chased the boys into the garage. It knew there would be liver inside if it was able to get to the human boys. Every living thing had a liver. It walked up the side of the house looking for an opening. It moved quietly on the roof until it found the chimney. It crawled up the chimney and looked down into the opening. It then began its descent into the house. It squeezed down to the size of the flue and crawled down the pipe.

It stuck its eye out into the fireplace to see if the boys were there. The creature didn't see them. It came out of the fireplace resuming to its normal size. It walked down the hallway smelling the areas as it went. It could smell human at the end of the hall, but the door was closed. It tried pushing it, but it wouldn't open. Orlando's mom thought she heard a noise outside in the hallway.

"Are you boys out there?" she said. There was no answer.

The creature left the hall and started up the stairs. Francine Gomez opened her bedroom door and looked out. The hall was empty. There were no lights on. She left the door ajar so she could hear and went back to bed.

The creature was at the top of the stairs when Spencer came out of the bedroom and across the hall to the bathroom. The creature hurried but was too late as Spencer closed the door. The creature could smell liver on both sides of the hall. He waited to attack once a door was opened.

Spencer had an upset stomach from eating too many Oreos. He had finished the whole bag during the movie. He sat on the toilet with a big tummy ache. The creature waited. The creature lost patience and began pushing against the door.

“Hey, I’m in here!” Spencer cried out. The monster then threw itself against the door, trying to knock it down.

“Cut it out!” Spencer screamed as he sat there naked with his underwear around his ankles.

Orlando and Jonathan were woken by the screaming. Orlando asked, “Was that Spencer?”

“Sounded like him. Where is he?”

The boys jumped out of their beds and hurried to the door. Orlando flung the door open. The creature turned its eye toward them. The hallway nightlight lit it up. It glowed gold. Orlando slammed the door before the creature could strike. The creature turned his attention to Orlando and Jonathan. Two livers were better than one, it thought. The creature pushed against the door. Orlando locked it and the two boys leaned against it with all their might.

Orlando reached for the bear spray that was lying on his desk. The parents in the neighborhood made their children carry bear spray while playing in the woods, even though there had never been a bear attack near the town, but there were bears seen every so often. Orlando then ran to his window and opened it as wide as he could get it.

Francine Gomez heard the screaming and was calling out, “Boys, what’s with all the racket?” As she made her way towards the stairs, she slipped on the slime that had been left behind by the monster’s sucker feet and fell to the living room floor.

Orlando opened the door after hearing his mother. He didn’t want the monster to attack her. The monster grinned at him and its eye extended to within two feet of his face. Orlando lifted the bear spray and fired it into the eye.

The boys had never heard such howling. Orlando and Jonathan moved away from the door and the thing made a hasty exit out the window, and went down the side of the house, screaming bloody murder as it left.

The boys heard it howling as it made its way back to the woods.

Folks the next day at church would ask their neighbors if they heard the wolves in the woods.

Spencer finally came out of the bathroom.

"Did you see it?" Jonathan asked Spencer.

"No! But it scared the poop out of me! I thought it was going to break down the door."

Orlando's mom appeared at the door of his bedroom, "What is going on? And what is all the slime on the floor? I nearly killed myself!"

"Mom, I think we need to talk," Orlando told her.

# Chapter 4

Orlando's mom sat on the chair at his desk while the boys sat on the bottom bunk facing her.

"What's going on?" she said. Orlando and his friends knew she was mad and serious.

"You won't believe this." Orlando started.

"Try me."

"This afternoon we were riding our bikes down the street when this monster, or creature started chasing us."

"Boys."

"It's the truth," Jonathan pleaded.

"We made it into the garage and dropped our bikes where you saw them. It tried to get under the door."

"It's the reason Orlando closed the garage door as soon as you pulled in," Jonathan told her.

"It's why we stuffed the cushions and pillows in the fireplace. To keep it out," Spencer told her.

"You said something about a monster earlier," she said.

"You didn't believe us. I don't blame you," Orlando said.

"What does this monster look like? You sure it's not a bear or something from the woods?"

"It's around six feet long with T-Rex arms that pop out of its body," Spencer started.

Jonathan added, "It grins like a human and has small, pointed ears."

"It had a lot of legs and suctioned feet. It can climb walls and windows," Orlando said.

"It's kind of an orange, yellowish color," Spencer said.

"Oh! This is the worst thing," Orlando said.

"There's a worse thing?" she asked.

"Yes. It only has one eye, and it pops out of its forehead and extends three or four feet. Mom, I know it's hard to believe. But it's true. That is why I didn't want to take the cream back to Mrs. McGill. We were scared."

"Okay. What is the slime on the floor?"

"It leaves a slime wherever it goes. We think from its feet," Spencer said.

"Were you boys pushing on my bedroom door earlier?"

The three boys looked at her and at each other. Orlando then said, "No. That means it was trying to get you also."

"Do you know how it got into the house? Everything was locked up. I checked before going to bed."

"I bet it was the fireplace," Spencer said.

"We can follow the slime," Orlando told her. The four of them exited the bedroom and went down to the living room and turned on the lights. There were slime prints from the hallway directly to the fireplace.

"It must be able to change size if it came down the chimney," Orlando told them.

*Mrs. Gomez believed the boys,* or at least some version of what they told her. They tended to exaggerate so much. But she could tell they were scared, and she couldn't see them putting the slime on the floor.

*The creature* tried wiping the bear spray from its eye, but the small arms were no help, even with extending its eye. Its eye hurt worse while it was extended.

*"We'll clean* the slime in the morning. We better get some sleep, if we can," she said. "Before going to bed, stuff the cushions and pillows back into the fireplace.

The boys quickly did it, knowing how to do it the second time. They moved the recliner back in front of the cushions and headed back to bed. Orlando looked at his phone. It was three-thirty.

After lying there for a half hour, Jonathan asked, "How are we supposed to get back to sleep? I'm wide awake."

"Me too," Orlando said.

They heard Spencer gently snore.

Sunday

*Around five,* Orlando slipped out of bed. Jonathan followed him. He went to the laundry room and got a few rags and a bucket. He put some water in the bucket and the two boys cleaned the slime from the floors.

The slime was sticky and hard to get up. Orlando found a sponge that helped in the process. By seven they had it done except for his room. They would wait until Spencer got up, which they knew might be a while. They went outside and cleaned the front window. They could see slime marks on the front bricks leading to the roof. Orlando would try to spray it off with the garden hose later. They went around to the backyard to look for more slime. It seemed like it only left slime behind when it was climbing or on hard surfaces.

As they stood looking, they heard someone shout, "Oh, Dear God, no!"

Orlando recognized Mrs. Johnson's voice. They ran through the Gorman's yard to the next house where Mrs. Johnson lived. She was an older widowed lady, maybe 85, who lived with her cat, Fluffy. She had always been nice. She made cookies for Orlando when he helped her with things. He had helped her a lot with her computer.

They ran to where she stood. Her cat, Fluffy, laid dead at her feet.

She looked up at the two boys and cried out, "Who would have done this to Fluffy? He wouldn't hurt a mouse."

Orlando doubted that statement but agreed that Fluffy was a nice cat. It looked like her stomach had been ripped open.

"I'm so sorry, Mrs. Johnson."

"Me too," Jonathan said.

"Why would someone do this?"

"It looks like some animal did this. Maybe a coyote," Orlando suggested.

"A coyote would have eaten all of her," Jonathan said.

Mrs. Johnson began crying harder.

Their neighbor, Mr. Gorman, was out getting the morning paper when he heard the sobbing coming from Mrs. Johnson's backyard. He went to investigate. He rounded the corner and saw the boys and Mrs. Johnson sitting on the patio.

"What's happened?" he asked as he approached.

"Somebody killed Fluffy," she sobbed.

He came closer and bent down to take a better look. He then looked at the others and said, "I found a dead squirrel at the side of the house that was killed the same way yesterday when I came home. Whatever killed them only wanted the liver."

This was too much for Mrs. Johnson who had taken a seat on the patio. She tilted her head between her knees and wept.

"I'm so sorry," Mr. Gorman said.

Orlando figured he knew what had killed the animals but didn't know whether to say anything or not. He had no proof of it and didn't want to panic them and the whole neighborhood.

She paused her crying long enough to say, “I heard the wolves howling real close last night. It had to be them. The lousy killers!”

“I heard them too. But I don’t think they killed Fluffy. They would have taken the meat with them,” Mr. Gorman said, confirming what was said earlier. “Could have been a large bird? But what only takes the liver?”

“Would you like for us to do something with Fluffy?” Orlando asked.

She wiped her tears and said, “Would you boys dig a deep grave back in my flower bed and bury her for me? I’ll find a nice box for her,” she said.

“Sure. We’ll do that for you and Fluffy,” Orlando said. “I’ll go get a shovel.”

Orlando and Jonathan left, heading to get a couple of shovels. Francine had a large shovel and a smaller garden flower shovel. They opened the garage door and found them. Orlando punched in the numbers and closed the door as they left.

They found a good spot in the flower garden that was bare of flowers and began digging. Mrs. Johnson’s flower bed backed up against the woods that edged their backyards. Both boys had bear spray in their pockets as they dug. They kept looking toward the woods. It took them around a half hour to get the hole three feet deep, not being expert shovelers.

Orlando went back up to the house and knocked on the back door. Mrs. Johnson opened the back door and handed him an old mixer box.

“I think that will do,” she said.

“Do you want to come out and say some words, Mrs. Johnson?”

“I’ll be out in a minute,” she said.

Orlando bent down and picked up the cat. It was already stiff. He placed it in the box and closed the lid. He walked it back to the grave they had dug. Mrs. Johnson opened the door. She had changed into a

Sunday dress for the funeral service. Jonathan ran over and helped her through the yard.

"You boys are so nice. Not like that Spencer brat."

Orlando and Jonathan had a hard time not laughing.

"He has his moments," Orlando said.

Orlando placed the box into the bottom of the hole and stood.

Mrs. Johnson looked down into the grave and said, "God, take care of Fluffy until I get there." She turned and walked away.

Jonathan helped her back to the house leaving Orlando to start filling the hole. He had almost forgotten about the creature until he heard rustling in the woods. He stood up straight and looked deep into the woods trying to see something. He couldn't see anything even though he still heard it. He hurried his shoveling as Jonathan returned.

"I heard something in the woods. Listen," Orlando said.

"Let's get this done," Jonathan said, as he started throwing dirt as fast as he could. As they were finishing up, Orlando looked to his right and saw an oblong object looking like a walnut, but he knew it wasn't. He picked it up.

"Let's get out of here," Jonathan said.

The boys ran all the way back to Orlando's house. They found Spencer at the kitchen table eating biscuits, bacon and eggs. Mrs. Gomez was standing at the stove.

"You boys want eggs?"

"Yes, please," Jonathan said.

"Scrambled, please," Orlando answered.

"Where have you boys been?"

"We've been burying Mrs. Johnson's cat, Fluffy," Orlando said.

"Fluffy died? I liked Fluffy," Spencer said.

"How old was the cat?" Orlando's mom asked.

"He didn't die of old age," Jonathan said.

"He was killed last night," Orlando said.

Spencer dropped his fork to the floor.

"What killed him?" Francine asked.

"What do you think?" Jonathan said.

"This is the other thing. A squirrel was killed between our house and the Gorman's. Mr. Gorman found it last night. He said they both had their livers removed and that's it," Orlando said.

Spencer sat there with his pie hole open, eggs falling from his mouth.

"We need to call a neighborhood meeting. We need to let people know about this monster," Orlando's mother said. "Orlando, finish these eggs."

She went to the phone and called Mr. Dunbar, the head of the community board.

"John here," he answered.

"John, this is Francine Gomez. I need to ask for a community meeting as soon as possible. This is urgent."

"What did McGill do now?" he asked.

"This has nothing to do with Sam. We were attacked last night in our home."

"Is everyone okay? Who was hurt?"

"We avoided injuries. But we need to warn the community."

"Who attacked you?"

"I'd rather wait till the meeting to discuss it."

"I'm just leaving for church. Others will be in church also. It's not a good day for a meeting. We'll talk later." He hung up.

She looked toward the heavens for strength to not blow up in front of the boys. She returned to the kitchen to see Orlando serving the eggs.

"What did he say?"

"Not today. He was busy."

"Too busy to talk about a monster in the community?"

"I didn't exactly tell him about the monster. I don't think he would have believed it. But I did tell him we were attacked. If it's not a complaint about Sam McGill, he doesn't want to hear it."

John Dunbar and Sam McGill had a running feud. They had run against each other for president of the community board. Words were said that cut each other to the bone. The scars had never healed.

John was always looking for a reason to kick Sam out of the neighborhood. If John knew Sam had unleashed the monster into the community, it would have made his day.

Francine changed the subject. "Mrs. Johnson must be heartbroken. I'm going to visit her and try to comfort her. I have to be at work at noon. What are you boys going to do today?"

They all shrugged.

"If we go outside, we'll have the bear spray handy. The creature didn't like it," Orlando said.

"It might be best to stay inside today," his mom told them.

"That's my plan," Spencer said.

"I'm going to see Mrs. Johnson."

"Take bear spray," Orlando told her.

She opened the drawer of the stand next to the front door and took a cannister of bear spray out and put it in her pocket. The entire drawer was filled with bear spray.

# Chapter 5

Francine opened the front door and looked both ways before stepping outside. She walked across the yard on the grass and continued to Mrs. Johnson's house.

She knocked on the door and waited. She rang the doorbell as she looked behind herself. Every sound unnerved her. Ruth Johnson finally came to the door and opened it.

"Hi, Ruth. Can I come in?"

"Of course, Francine. Please."

"The boys told me about Fluffy. I am so sorry." Ruth led her into the kitchen, and they sat at the table.

"I don't know what might have killed her. I am so upset," Ruth told Francine. "I think it was the wolves or the coyotes. They are getting terrible."

"Can I fix you some tea?"

"Yes. That would be nice." Francine got up and headed for the tea pot. She filled it and placed it on the stove to heat.

"Where do you keep your teabags?"

"Just to the right of the stove. Earl Grey would be nice," Ruth said.

She took her seat again as she waited for the water to boil.

"It was so nice of the boys to help bury Fluffy. It's still hard to believe she's gone."

"I know it's soon, but you should get you another cat."

"I don't know. It would be unfair for me to leave her when I die. I'm not getting any younger."

"You have a lot of life left, Ruth. I would take the cat if that should happen," Francine offered. Francine had never actually liked cats and even thought she was allergic to them, but she saw how unhappy Ruth looked.

"How would I even find one?"

"We can look in the paper. Or, doesn't Jonathan's mother volunteer at an animal shelter? You could rescue an older cat."

Ruth's face brightened at the thought of giving a home to a homeless cat.

"If you want, I could talk to her and ask her if they have many cats to pick from. I could take you there tomorrow morning," she offered.

"Okay. That is awfully nice of you," Ruth said.

The teapot went off.

***The creature*** had found a cozy spot in the woods and settled down to sleep. Its eye still stung. Its instinct was to sleep during the day and hunt at night. It was safer to move in the dark. The thing had perfect night vision. It didn't know where it came from or what it was doing there. It just existed and went by instinct. It constricted into a foot long caterpillar looking thing as it rested and slept between two large rocks.

***Rufus Langley's wife*** had died three years earlier. Rufus was sixty-eight and set in his way. He had never looked for a new wife, if he had, perhaps what comes next wouldn't have happened. He was satisfied with a quiet life in the community and hikes in the woods looking for different types of birds.

After eating a late breakfast, he remembered the objects he had found in the woods. He decided to go down and crack them open. He had found three of them. He figured if they were nuts, he would feed them to the squirrels that visited his backyard.

He went down the basement steps after closing the door behind him and went into his workshop. He grabbed his hammer and walked over to his worktable. He found that the three shells were already open. He stood there confused. He knew they weren't open when he put them there. He lived by himself. No one else could have opened them.

The three creatures slithered closer behind him as he stood there looking at the empty shells. They had grown to four feet in the light and dampness of the basement. Rufus placed the shells in his left hand to throw in the trash and turned to go back upstairs. The three creatures extended their three eyes up into his face. He screamed, grabbed a hatchet off the worktable and swung, cutting the eye off one of the creatures. The eye rolled under the worktable. The thing howled loud enough to burst his eardrums. Then, the two other creatures jumped on him before he could swing again and fought over his liver, while the third kept running into things in the basement.

Five minutes later, the creature without an eye shrunk back into the size it was when it was in the shell, withered and died. The eye under the worktable blinked.

***Francine returned home*** and got ready for work.

"How is Mrs. Johnson?" Orlando asked.

"She's doing better. I think I convinced her to get a new cat. Jonathan, could you ask your mom if they have a cat at the animal shelter that might be a good fit for Mrs. Johnson?"

"Yeah, I'll let you know."

"You boys be careful. If you go out, carry your bear spray," she said.

"Love you, Lando," she said as she hugged her son. "Close the garage door."

Francine was so tired after the night she and the boys had. Sleep never came as she kept hearing every creak and sound inside and outside the house.

After she had left, Orlando said, "Let's go swimming at the pool."

"Yeah, there may be some pretty girls there. Maybe Rhonda Lewis will be the lifeguard," Spencer said excitedly.

Rhonda was a seventeen-year-old blonde-haired beauty with a great body. The older boys that went to the pool were there for only one reason – Rhonda Lewis. She lived beside the pool on Ash Street, down the street from August Simms.

"What about the monster?" Jonathan asked.

"There will be plenty of people there. We should be okay. We can't hide forever," Orlando said.

"I'll go change into my trunks," Jonathan said.

"Me too. Pick me up on the way," Spencer told them.

"Take your bikes out the side garage door and lock it behind you," Orlando told them. He went up to his room, and while he was changing, he saw the odd-looking nut on his desk. He picked it up and hit it against the edge of his desk. It left a mark on his desk. "That was stupid," he said to himself. But it wasn't like it was the first scratch on the old desk. They had bought it years ago at a garage sale. He dropped the thing back on his desk, grabbed a beach towel and took off.

Jonathan lived only a few houses from Orlando on Oak Street. Orlando took his bike out the side door, locked and closed the door. He looked around the area for the creature and then took off. When he rode into Jonathan's driveway he yelled, "I'm here!"

The front door opened, and Jonathan's mother stepped out onto the porch. "Hello, Mrs. Miller."

“Hello. Orlando.” She had always liked Orlando. He was nice and courteous. She had no idea how they became friends with Spencer, who at times was discourteous and, how do you say it nicely, gross.

“Jonathan told me about Mrs. Johnson’s cat. Tell your mom we have a couple of cats that might be just right for Ruth,” she said.

“Thank you. I’m sure Mrs. Johnson will be happy to hear that.”

“I’ll be at the shelter in the morning if they want to come and take a look.”

“Do they have any German Shepherd puppies yet?”

“I doubt it, but I’ll look in the morning.”

Orlando had always wanted a German Sheperd pup. He knew the dogs were loyal and smart. He also thought it would be a good guard dog for his mom and him.

“Come in the morning with your mom and we’ll look and see what we have available.”

“Okay, thanks,” he said as Jonathan burst out the door and jumped on his bike, his beach towel over his shoulder.

“See you later, Mom.”

“Will you keep an eye on Julie if she comes to the pool?”

“Sure,” he answered as they pedaled away.

As they rode toward Spencer’s house, which was around the corner on the right side of Maple Street, the main road in the neighborhood, they saw August riding toward them. When August stopped, they stopped.

“We’re going to the pool if you want to join us,” Orlando said.

She couldn’t have smiled any bigger. “Okay. I’ll meet you there.”

The boys continued as August turned around and headed home to change. They were soon turning into Spencer’s driveway.

“We’re here!” they both shouted out. This was the boys’ usual notice of arrival.

Spencer came out of the house wearing bright orange swim trunks with lemons and limes dotting the fabric. They came down to his knees.

"What are you wearing?" Jonathan asked as he laughed.

"They look like kitchen curtains from seventy years ago.

"Snazzy, huh?" Spencer said, not paying attention to his friends' jabs.

"I think it could be protection from the creature. No living being should wear something like that," Jonathan said.

"I can tell when someone is jealous," Spencer told him.

Spencer hopped on his bike, which had been thrown in the flower bed, breaking a limb off a rosebush. When they arrived, they parked their bikes in the bike rack and took off for the gate to the pool.

"Do you see Rhonda?" Spencer asked.

"No," Orlando said. "Why do you care about Rhonda?" The other two boys just looked at him.

And then it happened! Rhonda came out of the dressing room and walked right past them. Her breasts bounced as she walked. Her swimsuit was skintight, and a portion of her butt cheeks was showing as she swung by. The boys stood there staring.

She then turned and said, "Hi, Jonathan, Orlando."

"Hey, Rhonda," they spurted out.

After she was gone, Spencer said, "What am I, chopped liver?"

"I'd be careful saying that. We think the creature likes liver," Orlando told him.

Spencer looked at his friends and asked, "Do you think we're safe outside?"

"I don't know," Jonathan answered.

"We haven't seen it this morning," Orlando said.

They grabbed three of the lounging chairs near the lifeguard stand and draped their towels over them. Orlando then went to one of the diving boards and did a "Cannonball!"

Jonathan and Spencer followed him. The water was refreshing. It was nice doing something other than worrying about the monster that had entered their life. A half hour later, Jonathan's mother dropped off his sister, Julie. She quickly found friends to play with. August Simms arrived in a pink bikini.

August was a very pretty girl. Her skin was mocha colored. Her mother was white, her father, African American. She was thin and beginning to blossom. She had curly dark hair down to her shoulders. The boys couldn't help but look at her. She sure looked more grown up here at the pool than when they saw her riding her bike up and down the street.

Orlando had never been interested in having a girlfriend. He enjoyed his friends and sports, and games. But in this instance, he thought maybe a girlfriend wouldn't be a bad thing.

"Hi, Orlando, Jonathan. I finally made it," she said. The boys were taking a rest on the loungers at that moment.

"Would you like for me to find you a chair? I can drag it over and you can join us," Orlando offered.

"Sure. Thank you," August said.

She was thrilled that he had invited her to join them. The pool was crowded that afternoon, and it took some effort for Orlando to find an empty chair. He found one at the end of the pool and picked it up and carried it to their spot and placed it beside him. This made August's trip to the pool worthwhile.

"Did you hear about Mrs. Johnson's cat?" he asked her once she was settled.

"Fluffy?"

"Yeah. She was found dead this morning."

"Mrs. Johnson?!"

"No. No. Fluffy. He had been attacked by something last night. Mrs. Johnson asked us to bury the cat in her flower bed."

"That's awful. It was a friendly cat," August said.

Apparently, Rhonda Lewis heard our conversation from her lifeguard stand and she said, "Fluffy was killed?"

I looked up and said, "Yeah, Mrs. Johnson thinks a coyote or wolf did it."

"What do you guys think?"

"I think it was something else, because whatever killed it, left the body behind."

"Maybe it died of old age," August offered.

Jonathan then said, "No. It had been attacked, because it was slit open and its liver was missing." Orlando wished Jonathan hadn't said that. Jonathan regretted saying it as soon as he said it.

"The only thing it took was the liver?" Rhonda said. She got down from her lifeguard stand and was now sitting on Orlando's lounger with her butt up against his legs. He pretended not to notice. But August noticed.

"What would do that? Who knew the liver was missing?" Rhonda asked.

"Our neighbor, Fritz Gorman, is a pharmacist at the hospital, and he knows anatomy. He found a dead squirrel between our houses also and the same thing had happened to it," Orlando explained.

"But what would just take a liver and leave the rest?" Rhonda asked.

"That's the question," Jonathan said.

"That is just creepy," August said.

The boys wanted to tell them about the monster that they had encountered, but they knew they shouldn't. It would spread and cause panic. Suddenly they had water splash all over them. They looked up to see Spencer at the side of the pool smiling.

"You look really pretty today, Rhonda," Spencer said.

"Maybe, until you got my hair wet," she told him and headed back up on her stand.

"Sorry!" Spencer yelled out. "But you're a lifeguard!" he added.

He then said, "Let's have a chicken fight."

Orlando looked at August and she said, "Okay."

Orlando said, "August and me against you two."

Jonathan cried out, "You don't stand a chance."

They jumped in the water beside Spencer.

"I'm on top," Spencer said.

"No way. I'm on top," Jonathan argued.

"We'll take turns," Spencer said.

Jonathan and Orlando knelt under the water while Spencer and August climbed onto their shoulders. Jonathan came up spitting water.

"You almost drowned me," Jonathan said, while wiping the water from his face.

"Better than being eaten by a monster!" Spencer yelled out.

August was so excited to be on Orlando's shoulder with his hands on her legs she ignored Spencer's comment. She couldn't believe it was happening. She liked Orlando so much, but he had never really seemed that into her. Maybe it was changing, she thought.

The chicken fight began. Spencer and August locked hands and began pushing and shoving each other. Finally, Spencer lost his balance and Jonathan let go of his legs and he toppled back into the water. August held her hands up high in victory.

"They never stood a chance!" she yelled.

"My turn on top," Jonathan told Spencer. Spencer went underwater and Jonathan just stood there watching him struggle.

“I’m going to see how long he can stay down there,” Jonathan said. The three of them laughed. Within a few seconds, Spencer came crashing up out of the water.

“Hey, what are you doing?” Spencer sputtered.

“Okay, I’m ready now.” Spencer went back under, and Jonathan hopped on. Spencer stood and it only took one good shove from August for Spencer to lose his balance and fall backward throwing Jonathan off.

Orlando bent down so August could get off gracefully. She threw her arms around Orlando and yelled, “We’re the best.”

She quickly kissed Orlando on his lips. He backed away and looked at her.

“What was that for?” he asked.

“Oh, nothing. It was just a victory kiss.”

“Oh,” was all Orlando could say.

It was the first kiss he had ever had from a girl other than his mother. It was a quick kiss, but he thought maybe he would like another one, maybe a little longer next time.

Spencer was busy coughing and spitting water, but Jonathan saw the kiss. He decided not to say anything about them. But he was right, August did like Orlando more than just as a friend.

# Chapter 6

**Sam McGill** had finished mowing his neighbor's lawn and was walking in his backyard looking at a mockingbird that was in a tree mimicking other birds. They always fascinated him. The tree sat at the boundary of his side yard and the back yard of his neighbor on Maple Street. To get a better view of the bird, he moved to his right and whistled a bird-call. The mockingbird called out. Sam thought the bird was trying to mimic him.

He took another step to his right and stepped on something. He figured a rock. He looked down and saw another oblong nut-like object like he had opened the day before. He started to throw it into the woods and then thought better of it. He would smash it with his vise grip that was mounted on his worktable in his workshop. He placed it in his pocket.

Sam still couldn't figure out where they were coming from. He had lost a lot of sleep thinking about that, and about the thing that had come out of the object. He wondered why the boys had asked him if he had seen something strange in the neighborhood.

It was two in the afternoon and the boys headed home from the pool. August was sad to see Orlando leave. Orlando had told her before leaving, "Hey. Maybe we could hang out sometime."

That turned her sadness into happiness as she waved goodbye. Spencer said he was going home and taking a nap. He looked worn out.

As Jonathan and Orlando were making the turn onto their street, they heard a voice call out, "Hey, boys!"

They turned their heads to see Sam McGill motioning for them to ride over to where he stood.

Sam had never bothered to learn their names. He knew they once had told him, but didn't see a reason to remember them.

They turned around and rode up to him. They stood in front of him straddling their bikes.

"Yesterday, you asked me if I had seen something strange," he said. "Why did you ask me that?"

Orlando didn't know how to answer him. He figured Sam knew something. The creature had come out from between the houses close to Sam's house.

We need to tell someone, Orlando thought. "We had that creature we described to you chase us down the street. It came from between those two houses." Orlando pointed to the spot Sam had last seen it.

"We thought maybe you had seen it or something," Jonathan said.

"I did." He reached into his pocket and pulled out the unopened shell and held it out in the palm of his hand.

"I found one of those!" Orlando said.

"You did?" Jonathan questioned.

"Don't open it!" Sam almost yelled, making the boys jump.

"What's in it?" Orlando asked.

Sam hesitated, thinking whether to tell the boys or not, but they had described it already. Only their description had the thing a lot bigger.

He needed to tell someone, "I was able to pry a piece up and it broke off."

The boys were enraptured by his telling of how he opened the nut. They stayed quiet and listened as though Mark Twain was the orator.

"I peered inside, and this face was looking back at me. It grinned and then its eye popped out toward me."

"What did you do?"

"My neighbors wanted to kill it."

"Wait, other people saw it?"

"Yeah. John Smith, two doors down, found it, and asked me what it was. He was having a cookout with some friends."

"What did you do?" Orlando asked Sam.

"I put it on the ground and ran over it with the tire of my mower."

"Then why didn't it die?" Jonathan asked.

"It must have escaped the shell before I ran over it, because I thought I saw it going around the corner of the house, but I wasn't sure. The thing I saw crawling around the corner was a whole lot bigger," Sam explained.

"The creature grew to six feet long and chased us into Orlando's house," Jonathan said.

"It got into our house last night and tried to kill us," Orlando told Sam.

"What!? Did you kill it? You must have, you're standing here."

"I opened the window and shot it in its eye with bear spray. It screamed and went out the window," Orlando explained.

"Where did it go?"

"I don't know, but this morning we found a dead squirrel and Mrs. Johnson's cat, Fluffy, outside dead. The only thing taken from the bodies was their livers."

Sam stood there looking as though he was in shock.

He then asked, "How did it get in your house? Surely you had locked your doors."

"It came down the chimney."

"But by your description how could it do that?"

"I think the monster can change shape, or squeeze into smaller places," Orlando told him.

"I'm going to my workshop and smash this one. They need to be killed," Sam said. "You need to do the same with yours."

"Can we watch?" Jonathan asked.

"Yes. And you had better go get yours and we'll kill them both," Sam said.

"I'll be right back." Orlando took off to get the object off his desk. Jonathan followed Sam to his porch.

Orlando opened the garage and ran through the house and up the stairs to his room. The nut was still there. He grabbed it and the bear spray and hurried out of the house, closing the garage door behind him.

He rode his bike back to Sam's house. They stood on the porch waiting for him. When he walked onto the porch, he held out his hand with the object in it.

"Just like mine," Sam said,

They went through the front door. Patsy was sitting in a chair reading a magazine. "Hi, boys. What's going on?" she asked as they walked down the hall to the basement door. The boys waved at her.

"Work," Sam called out, providing no other explanation.

They made their way down the steps and to Sam's workshop. The shop was organized to where one might think he was obsessed with neatness. He walked over to the large vice on the edge of the table and placed his nut in it and tightened it to where it held the nut firmly in place.

"Do you have bear spray?" Jonathan asked.

"I've got some," Orlando said as he pulled it out of his pocket. The boys took spots on each side of Sam. Sam looked at them and asked, "Are we ready?"

"I'm going to do this fast. We don't want the thing escaping," Sam said.

He then began tightening the vice as fast as he could. The boys heard the nut cracking open and then saw a face emerge from the cracked opening. Sam tightened the vice harder. The face popped out of the shell and the eye extended out.

Orlando took aim and sprayed it into the creature's eye. It screamed loud enough to warn the creature inside Orlando's shell. The shell started moving. Sam kept tightening the vice. Finally, the eye drooped over and stopped moving.

"What is going on down there?!" Patsy yelled from the top of the stairs. "Are you torturing those boys?!"

"We're okay, Mrs. McGill!" Orlando yelled up the stairs.

"You sprayed my hand," Sam said.

"Sorry. Would you rather I didn't?"

"No, of course not. But that screaming is deafening," Sam said.

"That's the same way the creature screamed last night."

*The creature* that was napping between the rocks was awakened by the screams. Its tiny ears stood up and listened for more screams. There were none. It went back to sleep, waiting for nightfall.

*Sam placed the remains* in a paper bag and asked Orlando for the other one. The nut was still moving around in Sam's hand. "It's trying to get out," Orlando told the other two.

Sam quickly placed it in the vice and began tightening it as fast as he could. The nut cracked open before Sam could break it with the vice and the worm jumped out onto the table. It sat there and then part of it stood up and its eye extended toward them. Orlando began spraying. The creature screamed. Jonathan and Sam looked for weapons. Jonathan found a hammer hanging on a pegboard and started swinging down at the thing. Sam picked up a three-foot pipe wrench and tried to squash it. The creature kept moving and screaming.

Next thing they knew, Patsy was standing beside them with her hands over her ears and screaming, “What is that thing?!”

She started swatting at it with her fly swatter.

Orlando looked around for something to use while the thing hopped around on the table avoiding the tools. The monster had already doubled in size. Orlando picked up a drill case and slammed it down on the creature. The screaming stopped.

The four of them stood there looking at the case, wondering if the creature would slither out from under it. After a couple of minutes of silence, Sam lifted the case and found the squashed dead creature lying there. Sam found a paint scraper and scraped the remains off the table and put it in a paper bag.

Patsy asked, “What was that thing?”

All three of the guys said, “We don’t know.”

# Chapter 7

**Rufus Langley's** basement had two monsters trying to find a way out. They searched every inch of the basement trying to find an opening big enough that they could squeeze through. They had shrunk back down to earthworm size and had climbed up the cement walls looking for a crack or a hole they could fit into. They would keep looking until they had no energy to continue.

Rufus's body lay on the cold cement floor. He didn't have any family that lived nearby. No kids to check on him. His neighbors wouldn't worry about him. They normally went days without talking to him or seeing him. His body would lie there and rot.

**Orlando** made sure to be in the house an hour before darkness enveloped the neighborhood. Spencer and Jonathan did the same. Orlando made sure the cushions and pillows were still stuffed into the fireplace opening. He checked every window in the house to make sure they were closed and locked.

**Sam McGill** did the same thing at his house. He thought he should report the monsters to someone, but who would believe him? It would take something awful happening before the authorities would believe him, and then they would be skeptical. Little did Sam know; something awful had already happened a few houses from his. He knew Rufus, but not well. They had spoken a few times when they met on the trails in the woods. They both had a love for birds.

But neither of them was very social, so they usually kept their short conversations at hello and goodbye.

Sam had a hard time calming his wife after what she had seen. He had no explanation to give her. She begged him to call the police. "They will lock us up in the looney bin," Sam told her.

"At least we would be safe," she said.

*Francine Gomez* returned home at eight-fifteen that evening after her shift at the store. She found Orlando home alone watching TV. She was surprised to see him alone.

She told him, "I had hoped you wouldn't be here all alone."

"Spencer and Jonathan were here last night. They had to stay home. I could have asked Rhonda Lewis to come stay with me."

His mom laughed and said, "I'm sure you would like that."

"You could hire her to sit me," Orlando suggested.

"I've seen the way all the boys at the pool look at her. Maybe, I could hire Mrs. Johnson," she said.

"Oh, by the way. We're supposed to take Mrs. Johnson to the animal shelter in the morning. Mrs. Miller told me she thought there were a couple of older cats there she thought Mrs. Johnson would like."

"Good. We'll try to get there when they open. I'll call Mrs. Johnson." She picked up her cell phone and called while Orlando went back to watching a saved episode of American Ninja Warrior.

Orlando looked out the living room window and saw that it was dark. He wished he could have warned the neighborhood to keep their animals inside after dark. He had a feeling the creatures only hunted at night since they had seen no sign of them during the day, except for when Sam had opened the nutshell.

*The creature* came out of the woods and listened for the sound of living things that might have livers. It moved along the grass going from yard to yard searching and listening. It deposited urps as it went. One here, one there. Not really realizing what it was doing, only knowing it needed to rid its body of the things, like a human got rid of its body waste.

A backyard light came on. Its eye extended toward the light and then hurried out of the brightness to the next yard. The creature suddenly heard barking. A small dog rushed toward it and then stopped short when the creature's eye popped out toward him. The dog barked and growled. The creature grew bigger. The dog began to retreat, sensing he should fear the creature. The fearful pup wanted to yelp, but never got the sound out. The creature had surrounded the dog with its entire body, ripped the dog's stomach open with his T-Rex arms and talon like claws, and then tore out the liver and consumed it.

Joe and Marcie Perry would find their six-year-old son's dog that evening, and Marcus would cry.

*After watching* American Ninja Warrior, Orlando decided to go to bed. He was tired from the lack of sleep the night before and spending most of the day at the pool in the sun. He started up the stairs when he saw his mom outside her bedroom in the hall.

"Did you eat supper?" she asked.

"I made a sandwich."

"You want me to warm up some soup for you before bed?"

"No, thanks. I'm going to bed."

"Come talk to me for a few minutes before you do. I never get to just talk to you."

Orlando was tired, but he knew his mother needed to spend time with him. He turned on the stairs and headed for the kitchen. Francine put on a kettle for tea.

She sat at the table with him as the kettle warmed on the stove.

"Did you see any sign of the creature after I left?"

He didn't really want to, but he told her in detail how they had opened the two shells in Sam McGill's basement and killed the worms.

"Wow!" she said. "What does Sam think?"

"He's as lost as we are. He was the one who opened the first nut that unleashed the creature. He has no idea where it came from or what it is."

"Did anything else interesting happen today?" The kettle went off and she got up to pour her tea.

"August Simms kissed me," Orlando blurted out. He had no idea why he told his mom that. He had never kept secrets from his mom. But this wasn't really a secret, so why would he tell her.

"How did that happen?" she asked.

"We were playing chicken fights in the pool and she and I defeated Jonathan and Spencer and then she kissed me."

"What did you do?"

"Nothing. I asked her why she did it."

"Why do you think she did it?"

"Jonathan says August has liked me for a long time."

"Do you like her?"

"Yeah. I mean, I don't know, I suppose, kind of, yeah."

"Maybe you should ask her over to watch a movie with you some evening when I'm home. I don't want the two of you alone in the house when I'm not here," Francine told him.

"Okay, Mom."

"You can go on to bed, I can tell you're tired. I guess I'm tired too. I'll take my tea with me to bed."

He got up and went over and hugged her. She kissed his cheek. "Night, Mom. Love you."

"Love you to the moon and back," she told him.

"Love you a bushel and peck."

"And a hug around the neck," she finished the rhyme.

It didn't take long before both were sound asleep.

***The creature*** moved around the neighborhood looking for more liver.

***That evening, Joe Perry*** went out to search for their dog, Trixie. The dog never wandered off and would come running when called. Joe was worried. He walked around the backyard while calling out, "Trixie! Come girl!" He moved toward the rear of the yard and saw a hump of something in the yard. He then discovered it was Trixie.

Monday

***The next morning*** Orlando awoke, and his thought went to whether the creature had struck again. He went to the kitchen to make some eggs and toast. He went to his mother's door and knocked softly.

"Yes. Lando?"

"I'm making some eggs and toast. You want any?"

"That would be great. I'll be out in a minute."

He placed four slices of bread in the toaster and scrambled four eggs. He added a little milk to make them fluffier, a trick he had learned from his grandmother, his abuela.

He placed a little oil in the skillet and turned on the gas flame. By the time his mother arrived the eggs were ready. He placed the toast on the table along with jelly and butter.

"This is a treat. What did you do?"

"Nothing."

"What do you want?"

"Nothing." He didn't mention the German Sheperd puppy he was hoping to find at the shelter.

"I told Mrs. Johnson we would pick her up a little before ten," Francine said.

"I hope they have something for her," Orlando said.

At nine-thirty the doorbell rang. Orlando ran to get it. It was Jonathan. He came inside.

"Are you taking Mrs. Johnson to the shelter?"

"Yeah."

"Can I go with you?"

"Sure."

"I'll surprise Mom. Oh, yeah, there's a community meeting tonight at the meeting room."

Francine heard the news and asked, "How do you know that?"

He handed the flyer to her. "This was stuck on every mailbox."

Francine looked at it and said, "Seven-thirty. I'll try to get out early. We aren't very busy on Mondays."

"What are we going to tell them?" Orlando asked.

"I don't know."

"We asked for the meeting."

"I guess we tell them the truth. Make sure Sam McGill is going to be there to back us up."

"It's going to sound crazy," Jonathan said.

"I suppose it will," Francine said. "It's time to leave."

They drove into her driveway even though it was only two houses away. Mrs. Johnson didn't move very well, and walked with a cane when she was out.

Francine went to the door to get her.

She rang the bell and got no answer. She waited and rang it again. She got worried and started to go back to the car. The door opened and Mrs. Johnson said, "Sorry, I was getting my shoes on." Francine helped her down the three steps and into the car.

Once she was settled, she said hello to the boys, "Where is that scoundrel, Spencer?"

"Probably still in bed," Orlando said.

"Good," Mrs. Johnson said. Showing she was not a fan of Spencer. He got that a lot.

"I do appreciate you taking me to the shelter, but I doubt I'll find a cat to replace Fluffy. It will be hard to do."

"I understand. But we'll take a look," Francine said.

Francine backed out of the driveway and drove down the road and made a right on Maple Street. She saw Spencer sitting on his bike at the end of his driveway. When he recognized the car, he started waving at them to stop. Francine pretended not to see him and went past him. Orlando knew why she had done it, but he felt bad for Spencer. He'd hear about it later.

It was only a ten-minute drive to the animal shelter once they left the subdivision. "I still think the coyotes got my baby, Fluffy," Mrs. Johnson said on the way.

"It was a real shame," Francine said.

"Maybe the dingo ate your baby!" Jonathan said, quoting Elaine Benes in a Seinfeld episode.

Jonathan, Orlando and Francine laughed and laughed at the line once when they saw the show together one evening. Orlando wanted to laugh again, but felt it was inappropriate at the time.

"What ate my baby?" Mrs. Johnson asked.

"A dingo, maybe a dingo ate your Fluffy."

Jonathan wasn't helping. Francine and Orlando were about ready to burst into laughter.

"Oh, dear. What is a dingo?" Mrs. Johnson asked.

"It's a wild dog."

"Do we have those around here?" Mrs. Johnson asked.

"I'm not sure," Jonathan said.

"A dingo," Mrs. Johnson pondered.

Francine was so happy to see the animal shelter up ahead. She couldn't take much more.

"Here we are," she announced.

She parked and went around to help Mrs. Johnson out of the car. They went inside and were met by the lady who ran the shelter.

"Hello, how can I help you?"

"Good morning. This is Mrs. Johnson. She is looking for a new cat," Francine told her.

"I don't want a kitten. Too much trouble."

"Jill told me you were coming in. She's in the back. Let me get her."

Jonathan's mother, Jill Miller, came out and greeted them.

"I was so sorry to hear about Fluffy."

"Thank you. We think maybe a dingo got her."

Jill took a quick look at the boys and knew what they had done. She almost laughed.

"I think we have a couple of cats you might enjoy. They need a good home."

The animal shelter had a lot harder time finding homes for cats than they did dogs. The shelter was a no-kill shelter and at times cats spent years there.

"Boys," the manager said.

The two boys stayed back while Jill led Mrs. Johnson and Francine to the cat section. The cats were kept in cages.

The manager told them, "We just got a couple of German Sheperd pups in on Friday. Jill told me you were interested in one."

Orlando's face lit up. "Really?"

"We hardly ever get German Shepherd pups. Would you like to see them?"

"Yes, please."

As they walked to where they were, Jonathan asked Orlando, "Is your mom going to let you have a pup?"

He shrugged his shoulders.

"This is the first you might like. Her name is Mittens. I guess you can tell why." The black cat had four white paws and a white streak between her eyes. It was a beautiful cat.

"She's eight years old. She would be a perfect companion."

Mrs. Johnson reached for her and held the cat in her arms. The cat purred as she petted her.

"I'll show you the other one I think you'll like," Jill said. She reached for the cat to put her back in the cage.

"I'll hold her," Mrs. Johnson exclaimed.

Jill led them to another cage where a grey and white Tabby cat stood purring. The cat was almost identical to Fluffy.

Mrs. Johnson quickly handed the black cat to Francine and reached for the Tabby.

A Tabby cat has a white distinctive M-shaped marking on its forehead, stripes by its eyes and across its cheeks, along its back, around its legs and tail.

"It's Fluffy!" Mrs. Johnson cried out.

"Her name is Buttons," Jill told her.

"What a silly name. I'll change it to Fluffy."

"She's five and very friendly."

"I'll take her," she said. Then she watched as Jill took Mittens from Francine and headed for the empty cage. Francine sneezed.

"Wait. I hate to see her go back into the cage. I'll take both of them," Mrs. Johnson told her.

"Are you sure?"

"Will they get along with each other?"

"I think so. It might take a day or so to get used to being together and new surroundings. But I think it will be fine."

"Then I want both babies. I'll keep them inside away from those dingos."

"How much are they?"

"The adoption fee is fifty dollars. But since you're taking two, you can have them both for sixty. Is that okay?"

"Yes. Will you accept a check?"

"Yes."

"Where are the boys?" Francine asked, realizing they weren't around. "Probably looking at dogs."

"He had asked me about German Sheperd pups. We just got two in. It's the first time since I've been here that we've had them."

"He's wanted one for years," Francine said. "I'm not sure why a German Shepherd."

"They are very good with families. Good protection and so loyal. They are really smart dogs and can be trained to do almost anything," Jill explained.

Francine thought about the monster that had invaded their house two nights earlier. It would have been nice having the dog there.

"Lead me to him."

Jill showed them which way to go and took Mrs. Johnson to the front desk to pay for her new companions.

Francine walked between all the cages as the dogs barked at her. Some jumped up on their cages wanting to be petted.

Soon she rounded a corner and saw Orlando holding a pup in his arms. The pup was licking his face.

"What are you going to name him?" she asked Orlando.

"I'll mow yards to pay for his food and shots, Mom," Orlando pleaded.

"I've already said OKAY."

"Really?!"

"I'll send Jill back," the manager said as she headed to the front.

Jonathan was holding the other pup.

While Jill was telling Francine what a good pet a German Sheperd would make, she realized that she had promised Jonathan a dog when he was old enough to take care of it. Maybe now was the time.

JIll arrived back where the boys held the two dogs.

"I'm taking this one!" Orlando told Jill.

Jonathan looked up into his mom's eyes.

She couldn't say no this time, "Do you want him?" she asked her son.

"Yes, yes, yes!" he shouted.

"You won't let the dingo's get him?"

They all burst out laughing.

It was quite a ride home in the car with the two pups yelping and the two cats hissing at them. Francine was sneezing every fifteen seconds. The pups were trying to get to the front seat where the cats were.

"I'm off tomorrow afternoon. We'll go to the pet store and get supplies for your dog," Francine said before sneezing.

"What should I feed him today?" Orlando asked.

"I'm sure he would love hotdogs or boloney," she said. "You must train him to go outside and do his business. I don't want the house smelling like urine." She wasn't really worried about it because their house had all hardwood floors. The kitchen had a tile floor.

They helped Mrs. Johnson into her house with the two cats, Mittens and Fluffy. She was very happy.

"I can't tell you how grateful I am. Thank you," she said.

"My pleasure."

Orlando then said, "You should keep the cats inside until we find out what's killing animals in the neighborhood."

"I plan on that. These are inside cats," she said.

The two boys took their pups to the backyard to play with them while Francine got ready for work. She had just enough time to get there early enough to make up for the time that she would be leaving early for the meeting that evening.

# Chapter 8

***It wasn't*** long before Spencer arrived in the backyard. "Wow! Where did you get the pups?!"

"The animal shelter."

"Are they yours?"

"This one here is mine."

"And this one is mine."

"Is that where you were going this morning?"

"Yep. We were taking Mrs. Johnson to find a new cat."

"Your mom must not have seen me. I was waving for her to stop."

"I guess not," I said, not wanting to hurt his feelings.

"Have you named them yet?" Spencer asked.

"I'm still deciding," Orlando said. They're both boys.

"How about Megatron? That's a good strong name for a German Shepherd."

"Or Megadog?" Spencer continued.

Orlando and Jonathan laughed. Spencer was always good for a laugh.

"I'm thinking Storm. Yeah. I like Storm," Orlando said.

"What about you, Jon?"

"I'm thinking Laddie," Jonathan said.

"Laddie?" Spencer questioned. "What kind of name is Laddie?"

"You know. Like Lassie, except he's a boy, so Laddie," Jonathan explained.

"It's for sure unique. He'll be the only dog in the world named Laddie," Spencer said.

"Then that's it, Laddie boy," Jonathan said.

"Laddie and Storm. I like it," Orlando said. The pups began wrestling with each other.

Before leaving, Francine came out back and told the boys, "I'll see you guys at the community meeting tonight."

"Okay, Mom. Have a good day. And thanks for Storm."

"Storm?"

"His name."

"I like it. It's a good strong name," Francine said. She was happy to see her son so happy. It couldn't be easy being alone most of the time and living without a father. She was thankful for the community and his friends.

The day went by fast for the boys as they played with the pups when they were awake. They quickly tuckered out and took many naps during the day. The boys talked about the meeting while the dogs napped.

*Sam McGill* decided to go see John Smith before the community meeting. He had seen John arrive home after work. He rang the bell and waited. John came to the door.

"Hi. Sam, isn't it?" John's wife stood behind him.

"John and…"

"Connie," John said. "Come in."

Sam went in and sat on the living room couch. Connie sat on the other end while John took a seat in a recliner.

"Can I get you something to drink, Sam?" Connie offered.

"No, but thanks. I'll be quick. Are you going to the meeting tonight?"

"We hadn't planned on it. We figured it would be boring stuff."

"Not tonight. Remember the creature we found in the shell?"

"We'll never forget that. Ever figure out what it was?" John asked.

"Not exactly, but…." Sam went on and told them what all had happened since that evening two days ago.

The couple sat there stunned.

"You think the creature from the shell did all of this?"

"I do. I didn't kill it when I ran over it. It must have escaped beforehand."

"So, the meeting is about the creature?" Connie asked.

"Yes. Francine Gomez called for the meeting after they were attacked in their home Saturday night. We need to warn people that this thing is out there somewhere. I need you to confirm what we saw in that shell."

John looked at his wife and she nodded. "Okay. We will be there."

"Thank you," Sam said as he rose from the couch. Before leaving he asked, "Have you found any more of those nut-like things?"

"No."

Sam left and headed for his backyard. He searched the yard for more of the oblong objects. Finding none he went into the Nelson's yard and searched. Finding none there he went into John and Connie's yard and searched. John saw him through the window and opened the back door and asked, "What are you looking for?"

"One of those shells. I thought it might be a good idea to show people at the meeting what they look like."

"You're right. Okay." He closed the door.

Sam headed into the woods searching along the trail. It was dim in the forest. The sun was low in the sky, darkening the forest. He was about to give up when he found one on the side of the trail. He picked it up and put it in his pocket and hurried out of the place where he had always felt happy and at peace. Now, it felt creepy and scary to him.

**During the day,** if Francine saw anyone from the community at the grocery, she would tell them to make sure they came to the meeting, "It's very important," she would tell them.

The grocery store where she worked was the closest one to their neighborhood. It was also the nicest grocery in the town. She had gotten to know so many folks from the community from seeing them in the store.

She had no trouble convincing her boss to let her off early, especially since she had come in early.

***It was getting time*** to leave for the meeting. Jonathan and Spencer had gone home for supper. Orlando boiled a couple of hotdogs and he and Storm ate their supper. He walked outside with Storm while he searched for a spot to pee. He didn't have a cage to place the pup in. He would have to leave him alone in the house. He placed the pup in his room. And took everything off the floor and threw it into the closet. He put a rug on the floor for the pup to sleep on.

He then hopped on his bike and took off.

When he got there, he couldn't believe how many people were there. Usually no more than fifteen attended monthly meetings, most of them having some complaint to tend to. Tonight, there must have been a hundred people there. There were not nearly enough seats for everyone. Orlando stood in the back waiting for his friends to arrive. The first friend he saw was August Simms. She came in with her parents. She saw Orlando and went and stood with him.

"Do you know what this is about?" she asked.

"Yes. My mom called the meeting. It's partly about the dead animals."

Jonathan walked in without his mom and dad. He joined them in the back. Spencer arrived with his mother. His dad wasn't there.

"Are we really going to tell people?" Spencer said.

"Tell people about what?" August asked, looking at Orlando.

"The monster," Spencer said.

"The what?" she said as her stare at Orlando deepened.

"You'll hear about it in a minute."

John Dunbar walked up to the front of the room. At that moment Francine hurried inside. He saw her and motioned for her to come up front. They sat at a table with six chairs facing the audience. They were the only two up front at the table. I watched as Mom whispered something to Mr. Dunbar. Sam was sitting near the front, but John asked Sam to come sit with them. He went forward.

John turned on his microphone and said, "Thanks for coming this evening. This is the biggest crowd in our history."

"What is so important?" someone called out.

"Well, I'm not certain. Francine Gomez asked for the meeting, saying it was urgently important."

"I'm missing Jeopardy for this!" a lady yelled out.

"Before we get to the main reason we're here. Remember that your fees are due by the $15^{th}$ of the month."

A lady near the front raised her hand and asked, "What are we doing about those people who don't recycle?"

John answered, "Shirley, I can't make people recycle. I do urge everyone to recycle."

"You should fine people who don't recycle," she continued.

"Who would check to see if people are recycling? Do you want to do it?'

"No," Shirley said.

"Let's get to the main reason we are here. Francine, it's all yours."

Francine tapped on her mic to make sure it was on. She started, "This is going to sound crazy, but here goes. Saturday evening, my family was attacked in the middle of the night."

There was a loud gasp in the room.

"By a monster!" she blurted out. The room hushed and looked at her to see if she was serious.

"Are you saying somebody broke into your house? Why wasn't I told?" John Dunbar asked, looking upset at Francine.

"No, I know it's hard to believe, but a real-life monster came into our house and tried to kill us. My son, and his friends, Jonathan Miller, and Spencer Ash were in the house. It went into their room and my son sprayed its eye with bear spray. It screamed and went out the window."

John Dunbar covered her Mic and said, "Do you really expect us to believe this story?"

A few people started to get up and leave.

Sam McGill yelled out, "Wait! Hold on! She's telling the truth. Hear the whole story. John Smith is here with his wife and will verify what I'm going to tell you!"

Sam went ahead and told how the monster had been released and told the crowd what it looked like. He reached into his pocket and took out the nut-like shell he had found that evening.

"This is what it looks like," he said. He held the object up to show the crowd.

"Come here, Orlando," his mom told him.

August looked at Orlando as he went forward.

"Tell our community how you first encountered the monster."

Orlando looked out at the crowd and started, "Jonathan, Spencer and I were riding our bikes Saturday evening toward my house when the creature, or monster, whatever you want to call it, started chasing us. The thing was around six feet long. Like Mr. McGill told you, it had pointed ears, T-Rex-like arms, and a face with a wicked grin. It had humanlike teeth and only one eye that extended from the middle of its forehead."

A man stood up and said, "How could something that fit in that nutshell be six feet long within a short time?"

A buzz went through the crowd.

"We can't explain it," Sam said.

“The same monster squeezed down our chimney that night and attacked us. It’s the truth, why else would we come here with a story like this.” Orlando looked up to see that Fritz Gorman, the pharmacist, had arrived.

“That night, Mr. Gorman…” Orlando pointed to him, and he raised his hand, “found a dead squirrel between our houses. It was only missing its liver. The next morning, Mrs. Ruth Johnson found her cat, Fluffy, outside dead. The only thing missing was its liver. Mr. Gorman confirmed this.”

Joe Perry stood up and raised his hand and John said, “Yes, Mr. Perry.”

“We let our dog out last night before bed. He didn’t come back to the door, or when I called him. I went out and found him dead with his stomach ripped open. I don’t know if his liver was removed or not.”

People in the audience were getting restless as they listened and started to believe in the creature.

“We killed two of the monsters that we found in the nut shells in my basement yesterday.”

Sam’s wife, Patsy, stood and said, “They were hideous!”

“If you find these objects we need to destroy them before more creatures are released on our neighborhood. They are going to continue looking for food,” Sam said.

Orlando spoke up, “You need to seal any opening in your house. It came down our chimney.”

Most of the houses in the community had fireplaces for heat, being that it was Minnesota. One of the few that didn’t was Jonathan’s house.

John Dunbar asked, “How do you know it came in through the chimney?”

Orlando explained, “Its feet are suctioned. It climbs brick and glass and leaves slime behind. The slime trailed from the fireplace in our house. We now have it blocked off.”

One man shouted out, “I don’t believe a word of this. It’s like a crummy horror book.”

“That’s your choice, Blake, but how do you explain the dead animals?” Sam asked.

“Coyotes, wolves.”

“You know good and well they wouldn’t leave a corpse behind. They would eat the meat,” Sam argued.

Another one said, “We should call the authorities. The police.”

“We probably will,” John said.

John looked out at the crowd and asked, “Has anyone seen Rufus Langley? He never misses a meeting.”

“The flyer was still hanging on his mailbox,” Rufus’s neighbor said. “We haven’t seen him for a couple of days.”

“Did he go somewhere?”

“Don’t think so. He always has us check his mail and get his newspaper when he goes away.”

“We’d better check on him,” John said.

This scared the crowd. This did more to convince the crowd than any other thing had.

“Is there anything else?” John Dunbar asked.

“Remember to keep your pets inside at night,” Orlando said.

“Meeting is dismissed,” John said.

The folks looked scared and stunned at what they had heard as they left the meeting. Some hurried from the building to get home to their kids and spouses to make sure they were okay. I heard one man tell his wife as they were leaving, “This is the biggest load of crap I’ve ever heard. A one-eyed monster that eats liver.”

Orlando knew it was hard to believe. He kept thinking he would wake up and realize it all had been a nightmare.

***The creature*** had left its sleeping spot to search the neighborhood for a meal. It roamed the yards looking for small animals or a human to feast on. There were slim pickings tonight. It made its way toward the meeting spot. The creature saw many humans leaving the building, but it knew to be cautious. It left the area and went into the woods to look for food. A possum walked by him. It was the last place the possum would walk.

***John Dunbar and Sam McGill*** led a group of vehicles to Rufus Langley's house. They saw lights on inside the house. Rufus lived at the very end of Maple Street. If you drove straight down the street and didn't stop, you would run into his house. The cars parked in his driveway and around the cul-de-sac.

Francine and Orlando stayed around the meeting house to answer questions many of the folks had.

John led a few people up to Rufus's door and rang the bell. Sam McGill banged on the door with his fist.

"Something is wrong," Sam said.

"I've got a key to his house. He gave us a key to look after his plants when he's away," Rufus's neighbor said.

"Go and get it," John said.

He ran to his house and was back within a minute. He unlocked the front door and a few of the men went inside.

"Rufus! Rufus! Are you in here?" The house was a nice sized ranch with a full basement. They checked each of the rooms and found nothing.

The two monsters in the basement awoke from their sleep when they heard the voices calling out. They hid behind some boxes and waited.

They began to grow. The two eyeballs looked up over the boxes as they heard footsteps coming down the stairs.

"The light was left on down here," John Dunbar said. He led the way and called out, "Rufus, are you down here?"

He walked into the workshop and saw Rufus lying on the floor. His stomach ripped open.

"Oh! God, no!" he yelled out and then quickly looked around, scared for his own life. Sam came and stood beside him and looked down at Rufus.

The two monsters made their strike, coming around both sides of the boxes. John screamed and yelled, "Back upstairs!" The other three men began scrambling to climb the stairs. In his haste, one of the men slipped and fell causing the others to crash into each other.

Sam pulled his bear spray from his pocket and aimed it at the closest monster and sprayed it. The monster screamed, making the men stumble more as they tried to climb over the man who had fallen. The other monster was now nearing Sam. He changed his aim to it and sprayed. The two screams were enough to drive a man crazy. The monsters retreated to behind the boxes.

As Sam turned to leave, he saw an eyeball under the worktable. He could swear it blinked at him. When he got upstairs, he slammed the door shut and leaned against the door.

"Now we call the police," John said.

He looked at his phone and dialed 911 and reported the dead body.

Ten minutes later, the police and fire department were in front of the house taping off the scene.

The policeman in charge asked, "Who found the body?"

"I did, or we did," John said pointing to the men around him.

"Do you know the name of the victim?"

"Rufus Langley."

"Could you tell how he died?"

"Attacked by a mon…creature," Sam said. Sam thought monster sounded more unbelievable, Frankenstein…ish.

They described the two creatures in the basement and told the police they would need something to kill them. The police just looked at them in disbelief. "We have these," the policeman said, patting his gun.

"Then have at it," John told them.

*As Orlando and Francine* were on their way home, they saw the flashing lights in front of Rufus's house. They had seen the lights as they went by and figured something was up at the house. She parked on Oak Street, and they walked down Maple Street to the house. She saw Sam standing behind the tape and they went over to him.

"What happened?" Orlando asked him.

"We found Rufus in the basement, dead."

"Oh, no."

"The monsters?" Orlando asked.

"Yes. There were still two down there when we discovered the body."

"What did you do?" Francine asked.

He pulled the bottle of spray from his pocket and said, "Nothing you wouldn't have done."

"Poor Rufus. That's an awful way to go."

Orlando hated to ask, but he had to know, "Did he still have his liver."

"I don't think so. His stomach had been ripped open. I don't think I'll sleep another wink during the rest of my life," Sam said.

Orlando put his hand on Sam's shoulder. He turned and looked around for August but didn't see her in the crowd.

*Four policemen* went inside and searched the upstairs much like the men had. They drew their weapons and carefully went down the steps to the basement. So far, no large caterpillar creatures. They split up and began searching the basement.

"What is that smell?" one of the officers asked.

"Found the victim," one officer called out.

The senior officer then said, "Keep looking for the creatures."

They searched everywhere the things could be and found nothing. There were no creatures, no monsters, no things in the basement. One officer saw what he thought was a large marble under the worktable but left it there.

The four men gathered around the body.

"Someone really didn't like Rufus," one of them said.

"I've never seen anything like this."

"Call in the forensics team."

The two creatures' eyes still burned from the bear spray. It was as though their eyes had been drenched with the horrid stuff. They had shrunk back to their earthworm size and walked up an open lightbulb box and hid inside, afraid of being sprayed again.

The officers didn't realize that Rufus's body laid on top of the shriveled-up body of the creature that Rufus had killed.

The policemen went back outside to disperse the crowd, wait on forensics, and question the men who had told the wild story of creatures.

Sam and John were surprised to see the police come out of the house after not hearing any gunshots or screams. "What is going on?" Sam said, more to himself and John.

"We need for everyone to go home except for the men who found the body. Nothing to see or do here. Go on."

The crowd dispersed reluctantly. "What about the monsters?" someone yelled out.

"There were no monsters!" the senior officer yelled out.

Most everyone went home confused, but they locked all their doors, mad sure windows were shut and locked, and kept their pets inside.

*"This doesn't make sense,"* Orlando told his mom as they headed home. Sam said there were two creatures in the basement. They couldn't have just disappeared.

"Didn't you tell me you thought they changed shape?"

"Yes. That's it. If they shrunk back down to the size they were in the shell, they could've hidden anywhere. We need to go back and tell the policemen."

"No. They told us to leave," Francine said.

Orlando did as his mother said.

Orlando went into the house, got Storm from his room, and took the pup out to pee, staying close to the open door and keeping an eye out for the creature.

Sam, John and the three men who went with them into the basement were led into Rufus's dining room. They took seats at the table.

The chief of police had arrived. He began the questioning.

"Why did you guys break into this house?"

John Dunbar explained that the community had a meeting about the creatures that had been killing animals. He explained why they were concerned about Rufus and had come to his house to check on him.

The men described the two monsters again that had attacked them. The chief acted as though they all were crazy. The chief thought the men were trying to cover up what really happened.

The police let the men go back to their homes after questioning them. They had no clue as to what or who killed Rufus Langley.

*No one knew* where the creatures had come from. The creatures didn't know. They were controlled by instinct. Where their instincts came from was a mystery. Maybe aliens from somewhere out there in the sky. Maybe a new species that had sprung up by accident. Maybe a caterpillar that had fallen into chemicals.

They had the magical ability to go from an inch long to seven feet long in hardly any time at all, and then back again. What were they? How many of them were there?

# Chapter 9

**Orlando** let Storm sleep in his bed since he hadn't yet bought a dog bed. He had so many mixed emotions. He was happy because of the puppy, sad because a member of the community had been killed by the creatures, and scared because he knew it could happen to others, maybe his mother or him.

It wasn't very late, but he was already in bed even though he was wide awake. He was scrolling in his phone when he saw August's cell phone number. She had put her number in his phone during the meeting that evening. He placed his finger on her number and pushed.

"Orlando!" August said after one ring. "What's up?"

"I wanted to talk to someone," he said.

She was thrilled that he had chosen her to talk to. "Let's talk."

"Did you hear about Mr. Langley?"

"Yes. It's awful. Do you think the monster got him?

"Sam McGill said they did. The creatures attacked the men that went into the house."

"What?"

"Sam fought them off with bear spray and got out. The police couldn't find any sign of the creatures except for the body of Rufus."

"Where did they go?"

Orlando and August talked for another hour and a half about his different theories and thoughts. She was hanging on his every word.

"I guess I'd better go. I'm getting tired."

"Okay. See you tomorrow."

"Oh, August. Would ya...you want to be my gi...gir…girlfriend?"

"Yes. I'll be your girlfriend," August said with glee.

She hung up and called her best friend, April. There were also May, June, and Summer in the neighborhood.

She and April talked about Orlando and Jonathan mostly, never once talking about the creature that was roaming the neighborhood looking for liver. April had her eye on Jonathan, she hoped now that August had Orlando as her boyfriend, she might be able to see Jonathan more.

***The creature*** found nothing to eat in the neighborhood and went back into the forest and found an unexpecting skunk and consumed its liver.

***The forensics team*** was in the basement examining the remains of Rufus Langley and dusting for prints. One of the team looked under the worktable and saw the eye. He reached under the table with forceps and picked it up. He looked at it carefully and told the team, "Look at this."

They gathered around. One of the men asked, "What is that?"

Another said, "Looks like an yellow eyeball."

"Does Rufus have both his eyes?"

"Yes," another said. "His eyes wouldn't be yellow anyway."

"Then where did this one come from?"

No one had an answer. They put the eye in a clear plastic baggie.

Later, they loaded the body of Mr. Langley onto a gurney to take it away. One of the men in the rear said, "What is that on the floor?"

The remains of the eyeless monster were squashed on the cement floor. It had shrunk to be a foot long and was flat, like it had been deflated. They bagged it, all the while wondering what it was.

The team was scared and very eager to leave the basement behind.

Tuesday

*The next morning* Orlando awoke when Storm began licking his face. He quickly got up and took him outside before the pup peed on the floor or his bed. It looked like it was going to be a nice day. It was already in the mid-sixties and sunny. After eating breakfast and cleaning up, Francine asked if he was ready to go to the pet store.

"Can Jonathan come?"

"Of course."

Orlando knew that Jonathan probably needed supplies for Laddie.

A quick call confirmed that Jonathan wanted to go with them. His mother gave him money. She was thankful they were taking him so she could stay home with the other kids.

Francine had called Mrs. Johnson to see if she could pick up anything for her cats.

"That would be great. I already love my cats. I can't thank you enough for your kindness." She gave Francine a list of things she needed.

They stopped at a fast-food place afterward for lunch. The conversation turned to the creatures roaming the community.

"What are they going to do about the creatures?" Francine asked, knowing the boys didn't have an answer.

"I guess they could form a posse and hunt them," Jonathan said.

"I think it would be hard to find them. They could hide anywhere. The police couldn't find the two monsters in Mr. Langley's basement. They must have shrunk and hid."

"You think so?" Francine said

"We know they can change shape. When Sam first saw one it was worm size. A few minutes later they were six feet long chasing us down the street. It even came down the chimney."

"But we aren't positive it can shrink back to worm size," Jonathan said.

"You're right, but it makes sense," Orlando said.

After eating, they delivered the supplies to Mrs. Johnson. She paid Francine for the supplies and asked if she would like to come in and see the cats. Francine almost sneezed just thinking about it. "Not today."

**The coroner** didn't need to cut Rufus Langley open to see inside his body. The creatures had already done that. His report said that Mr. Langley's liver had been removed. He had died from the injuries sustained from the removal. The coroner also wrote about a slimy substance that was found on the victim. Much like the substance the forensics team had found on the basement floor and walls.

There was no explanation that could tell them what the squashed body was or what the eyeball had come from. They didn't think they could have been connected. They were wrong.

**The police's** only suspects in the death of Rufus Langley were Sam McGill, John Dunbar and the other three men who were in the house when the body was discovered. But even the police didn't believe they had done it. Who would have killed Langley to remove his liver? And why were other animals killed to have their livers removed? There were more questions than answers.

# Chapter 10

*The Woods* was a community built on an old farm that had run its course. Francine was one of the first to move to the community. After her divorce she wanted to move her son out of the city to friendlier, healthier surroundings. The houses were built pretty much inside a forest with the nearest town five miles away.

There was a pond not far away where the residents could fish. Not many of the residents of the community ever went there to fish since Minnesota was the land of ten thousand lakes. There were fishing lakes everywhere. Most fishermen headed for the bigger lakes, thus leaving the pond for the kids.

The forest around them had many trails which were either placed by the builder or made from the forest animals. Due to living in the middle of a forest it wasn't strange to see a moose or a bear wandering down the middle of the street every so often. Deer would bring their fawns to graze on the grass in the yards and munch on flowers. Apple trees lost all their low hanging fruit to the deer. Most residents accepted it and enjoyed watching the wildlife.

The community had a mixture of houses. It wasn't a cookie cutter subdivision. There were ranches, two story homes, brick homes, and wood houses that were painted in all assortments of colors. Each was unique and custom built. Francine had moved in seven years earlier and she and her son had watched the community build up around them. There were no empty lots now. The community is complete with a pool, a playground, a meeting house, a pond, and a 'creature'.

***While Francine*** had taken the boys to the pet store, Sam McGill was organizing a posse to search for any oblong nut-like objects in the community with the help of John Dunbar.

"We need to get rid of these things. You saw them."

"I agree," John Dunbar said.

John made a flyer, and he and Sam posted them on every mailbox. It told men that could be at the meeting house at six that evening that they were going out looking for the objects. They would search every yard, street and trail. They asked for men to bring bear spray and any guns they may have.

Orlando saw the flyer hanging on the mailbox when he went to check for mail. He read it and called Jonathan and Spencer. The three of them decided to join the search. When Francine was shown the flyer, she was totally against Orlando going.

"It says *men,* Orlando, not boys."

"We can search just as well as men can. It won't be like we'll be alone. We'll be with the men."

She knew her son wanted to help his community to keep others from being killed. She gave up the argument and agreed.

Jonathan, Spencer, August, April and Orlando played with the two dogs in the back yard. They taught them a few commands. The pups caught on quickly. Before their lessons were over, they knew the commands of sit, stay and come.

Orlando had called his girlfriend and invited her to come over, April showed up with her. April made no effort in hiding her feelings for Jonathan. She stayed by his side as he taught Laddie.

April was cute with strawberry blonde hair and green eyes. She was friendly and fun to be around. She lived down the block from August, across from the pool.

The boys walked to the meeting house that evening. On the way to the meeting house Spencer complained, "Now that you have a girlfriend, does that mean she and April are going to be hanging around us all the time?"

"Someone sounds jealous," Jonathan said.

"I'm not jealous. I just like the way things were."

"I'm not going to invite August all the time. All we had planned was training the dogs. I didn't see the harm," Orlando said.

"April has such a crush on you. Are you going to ask her to be your girlfriend?" Spencer asked Jonathan.

"No, she doesn't," Jonathan said.

Spencer and Orlando began laughing.

"What?"

"She was right beside you all afternoon. She acted more like the puppy than the puppy did, wanting to please you, trying to get your attention. It's a wonder she didn't lick your face," Orlando said. Spencer was cracking up.

"Okay. I admit she might like me. She's cute. Where's your girlfriend, Spencer?"

Spencer stopped laughing long enough to say, "I like to play the field."

"The only field you play is in your backyard," Jonathan told him as they arrived at the meeting house.

Quite a few men were milling outside the building. There were more men inside. A few women had joined them. One of the shells was being passed around so people knew what they were looking for.

John gathered the group of around twenty and said, "We'll split up in two groups. One group will search the yards on one side of the street and the other group the other side. Look carefully. We have bags for you if you find any. Sam will lead the other group. Comb all the grassy areas and flower beds. Spread out around three feet apart during the search. We'll start on Ash Street and work our way around."

Orlando and his friends went with Sam's group. They began on the right side of the street. The second house they searched was where Rhonda Lewis lived. While they were searching her yard she came out of her house and asked Orlando what they were looking for.

He described the objects to her, and she asked, "Have you found any?"

"Not yet," he told her. Rhonda wore shorts and a midriff top. She was so fine.

Spencer stopped searching and asked her, "Rhonda, would you be my girlfriend?" despite the fact she was five years older than him and going into her senior year of high school.

She smiled and then began laughing. She went back inside the house and closed the door.

"Slammed in your face, you big doofus," Jonathan told Spencer.

He took it in stride and said, "She didn't say no. She probably has to think it over."

"Yeah, sure. That's what she's doing," Orlando said.

"Found one," a man shouted from the backyard.

Both groups ended up meeting at August Simms' house. They joined forces. They found two more in the back yard. August was walking beside Orlando when one of the men found the two shells.

"That's so creepy," she said.

"At least they weren't open," Orlando told her.

By the end of the evening, they had found seventeen of the objects. It was getting dark, and they still had Elm Street to do. John said that he and Sam would do it tomorrow. Orlando told them that they would help. It was getting near nightfall, and everyone was anxious to get home before the dark enveloped the community.

Orlando and his friends walked with Sam as they made their way home. Sam was carrying a large bag with the seventeen objects.

Orlando asked Sam, "What are you going to do with the nuts? Smash them in the vice like the others?"

"No. I'm taking them to the funeral home and having them incinerated," Sam said.

"You mean like cremated?" Spencer asked.

"Yes," Sam chuckled.

"What are you going to do with them tonight?" Jonathan asked.

"I'm going to put them in the freezer."

*The forensics team* had gone back to Rufus's house to check the upstairs for prints and clues. One of the team had opened the basement door and forgotten to close it, not knowing that the two creatures were downstairs. Once it was dark outside the two creatures crawled out of the lightbulb box to look for a way to escape the basement again. They grew as they searched. They knew they needed to eat soon or die.

They went up the stairs to find the door open and went toward the only opening in the house, the fireplace. They squeezed up the chimney and onto the roof. From there they searched for prey to kill.

Spencer left his friends and turned into his driveway. It was dark by the time Jonathan and Orlando made their way onto Oak Street. They were hurrying to get home. Neither of them wanted to be out after dark. The creatures saw the two humans on the street and rushed to get off the roof and move through the backyards to cut them off. Just as the creatures got to the street, they saw Jonathan walk into his house. They took off after the other one.

Orlando didn't hear them behind him. They moved in silence as their feet scurried over the asphalt. Orlando turned into his driveway and looked behind him to see the monsters closing in on him. He ran as fast as he could to the front door and began punching in the code to the lock and frantically pressing the doorbell.

Francine was in the shower getting ready for bed. She was also worried that Orlando hadn't come home yet. The monsters were within fifteen feet of Orlando when he finally got the correct code entered and the door unlocked. He opened and closed the door just before the creatures got to him. He leaned against the door and took several deep breaths. Storm came rushing to him, jumping up on his legs. Orlando sat down against the door and let the puppy lick his face.

Orlando went to the phone and called Sam, "Two of the creatures chased me to my door. I just barely made it."

*The creature* that had been sleeping in the forest began his nightly hunt. As soon as he woke and began his hunt he pounced on a rabbit and ate the liver. It was an appetizer. He moved on into the back yards and searched houses for open doors or windows. He could sense that the chimneys had been closed off. He heard a dog in the distance and went toward the sound.

Storm was playing with Orlando in the living room. The creature moved to the bay window even though the front porch light was on. It was curious of the new sounds. The creature crept under the window and then extended its eye up over the ledge and peered at the dog.

Orlando was lying on the floor with the pup sitting on his chest. The pup saw the movement out of the corner of his eye. He turned toward it and the two of them stared at each other. Storm's ears stood on end. He slowly got off Orlando, who was watching an episode of Alone, and slowly moved toward the eye. He stood with his paws against the windowsill and stared eye-to-eye at the creature. He tilted his head as though trying to figure out what this eye was. The eye blinked and Storm barked.

Orlando turned to see what Storm was barking at and saw the eye drop beneath the sill. Orlando quickly stood and rushed to the window. Storm continued his barking. The creature moved along the bottom of the house and away. It remembered the stinging sensation from his last time at the house.

It moved to the back yard of Fritz Gorman's house and was met there by the two monsters that had escaped Rufus's basement. They looked at each other with no rejoicing or happy feeling at seeing one of their kind. They just moved off with a job to do – find liver.

The creatures moved around the edge of the woods as they searched and listened for sounds of living things. They knew that living things had livers in them. They left the end of Oak Street and went over to the backyards of Elm Street.

After the community meeting a man had left the meeting telling his wife that the whole thing was the biggest load of crap he'd ever heard. That same man was outside in his back yard with his dog, Freddie. He was sanding off the bottom of a door that he had placed on two sawhorses.

Freddie was smelling a rabbit trail at the edge of the woods when one of the creatures pounced on him. Sean turned to see why Freddie was whimpering to find two one-eyed monsters looking him in the face. They smiled, and before he could run or grab a weapon, they engulfed him till he suffocated and then took out his liver. The two creatures fought over Sean's liver after they had torn into the body's stomach to get to it, while the other creature ate Freddie's liver. Sean Bridges died believing in the creatures.

An hour later, Peggy Bridges wondered what was taking so long. She was ready for bed. She opened the patio door and looked out for her husband. She wouldn't get any sleep for the next few nights without medication.

The police arrived ten minutes later. The policemen looked down at the body and realized the same thing that had happened to Rufus had happened to Sean Bridges. The chief arrived on the scene after a call.

As he made his way back to the front of the house, he saw John Dunbar standing outside the yellow tape.

"You seem to show up at all the murders," the chief said.

"I live right over there," he pointed to the back of his house. "Who was murdered? Are you accusing me?"

The policemen knew that a person hadn't done the killing and mauling. It had to be an animal, or maybe the community was right in claiming that the murders had been by a monster that was roaming the neighborhood.

"Back here," one of the officers called out.

Chief Johanson followed the yell, along with other officers. The shout led them to where the policeman stood over the body of Freddie, the brown Peekapoo. The flashlight lit up the dog and showed that its stomach had been ripped open just like his owner.

The other officers turned on their flashlights and shone them into the woods. Scared expressions filled their faces. The creatures had moved further into the forest for protection after fulfilling their appetite.

"There is something here, Chief," one of the policemen said.

"No kidding, Lebowski."

***John Dunbar*** pulled his cell phone out of his pocket and called Sam McGill.

"I heard sirens. What's up?" Sam answered, knowing something was going on.

"There's been another killing at the Bridges house."

"Animal or human?"

"Human. Maybe both, unsure. Where are the shells?"

"In my freezer in the basement," Sam answered.

"Maybe we should turn them over to the police and let them open them. Maybe they'll take us seriously if they see the monsters for themselves."

"We're not sure what the freezer has done to them. They may have died in there. Perhaps we should find a couple more and turn them over," Sam suggested.

"Okay. Can you meet me in the morning at eight at the main trail entrance?"

"See you then."

The main trail had been built by the developers. It started at the park and continued all the way around the subdivision. It was a two-mile loop. Many folks walked the trail every day for exercise.

Once they had hung up, Sam looked at the time, it was ten. He called Orlando. He had grown fond of Orlando and Jonathan. He figured a few more eyes might help in the search for more shells to hand over to the police.

"Hello," Orlando answered. It was unusual to get a call at that time of night. He thought it might be August.

"Orlando, this is Sam. There's been another murder."

"What? Who? I heard some sirens."

"It's at the Bridge's house. Unsure who the victim is."

"I... I don't know them."

"They live on the cul-de-sac of Elm Street. What a nightmare!"

Orlando wasn't sure if Sam knew he had described a *nightmare on Elm Street* or not. He let it go.

"That's awful. I saw one of the creatures around a half hour ago outside our front bay window."

"That means they were roaming the neighborhood looking for victims," Sam said. "Anyway, John and I are meeting in the morning to look for a few more shells. I thought maybe you and Jonathan would want to help. We're going to turn them over to the police. Maybe they'll take our claims seriously if they open them up themselves."

"Okay. When?"

“Eight in the morning at the entrance to the main trail,” Sam told him.

“We’ll be there.”

Orlando hung up and then thought - wonder why they don’t give the shells we already found to the police. But then he figured they had their reason. He called Jonathan and gave him the news.

Jonathan said he would be there. “What about Spencer?”

“Sam didn’t say anything about Spencer.”

“He’ll be mad if we don’t include him.”

“Okay. I guess it will be alright.”

“I’ll call him,” Jonathan said and hung up.

Orlando lay in bed thinking about how the community had been the most peaceful place on earth. He and his friends had nothing to worry about other than riding bikes, playing in the woods and looking at the pretty girls at the pool. Now, there were residents and pets being killed and creatures roaming the community looking for more victims.

He wondered how they would get rid of the creatures, especially if they kept dropping shells creating more offspring. Orlando had a lot of trouble falling asleep. The puppy had been on his dog bed, but he jumped up on Orlando’s bed and nestled close to the safety of his best friend.

# Chapter 11

Wednesday

*The next morning* Orlando's alarm went off at seven. He felt like he had just gone to sleep. He got up and let Storm out to pee. His mother was in the kitchen fixing herself a bowl of cereal.

"What are you doing up so early?" she asked.

"Did you hear the sirens?" he asked.

"Yes. Do you know what it was?"

"Sam called and told me someone else had been killed over on Elm Street."

"Oh, no!"

"He didn't have details." Orlando went on and told her what the plan was for the morning.

"I don't know if I want you doing that," she said. "It's dangerous. Especially in the woods."

"I'll take the bear spray and Storm with me. Jonathan and Spencer are going also, and I can run faster than Spencer. I'm sure Sam and Mr. Dunbar will have guns."

"Even more reason I don't want you going."

"I'll be okay, Mom."

She sighed a big, long sigh and said, "Okay. Be careful. You're all I got."

"I know. I love you."

Jonathan and Spencer were telling their parents the same story, "But the other guys are going."

Francine had to be at work at eight that morning. She quickly ate and got dressed and left for work. After her shift at the grocery, she had to clean a house and wouldn't be home till late. She always posted her work schedule on a blackboard that hung by the fridge. Orlando left a little after her and rode his bike with Storm running beside him on a leash. The pup loved to run. He stopped at Jonathan's.

"You're taking Storm?"

"Yep."

"Okay, I'll take Laddie."

The two boys continued to Spencer's house. He was still in his pajamas.

"What are you doing, numbskull? We need to go," Jonathan told him.

"Sorry. I had a hard time getting up."

"If you're going, hurry, and don't forget your bear spray," Orlando told him.

They waited on the porch as long as they could and decided to leave him. They were turning into the pool area where the trail began when they heard Spencer yelling, "Wait up, guys!"

They parked their bikes at the pool's bike stand and walked to the trail's entrance. They saw John and Sam standing there waiting for them.

"You are late," John said, looking at his watch.

Orlando looked at his phone and said, "Four minutes."

"It's still late."

"It was my fault," Spencer said. It was big of him to admit it.

"I figured that much," Sam said. Sam then said, "Nice looking pups."

"This is Storm, and that is Laddie," Orlando told them. Sam bent down to pet them.

John then said, "We're going to walk the trail and look for the shells. Be careful. Have your bear spray out." Spencer checked his pockets and realized he had forgotten his.

Sam was carrying a rifle. John had a pistol in a holster on his waist, like a real cowboy, but he looked nothing like one. He looked more like a nerd with a gun.

"Why not give the police the shells we found before?" Orlando asked.

Sam answered, "The creatures probably died in the freezer. Or at least I hope they did. We want the police to see the real things."

"That makes sense," Orlando said.

They started their hike. As they walked looking at the ground Orlando asked, "Did you find out who got killed?"

Sam answered, "Mr. Bridges and his dog both were killed the same way as the others."

"That's awful," Jonathan said.

"Why aren't the police doing more?" Orlando asked.

"They're having a hard time believing that monsters are doing this. We're hoping the shells will convince them," John explained.

They had traveled around a half mile when Jonathan yelled out, "I found one!" He handed it to John, who put it in a ziplock bag.

"Good job," Sam said.

Spencer was lagging. "What are you doing back there?" Orlando asked him.

"I'm watching to make sure you guys don't miss any," he called out.

Orlando asked, "Where do you think the monsters go during the day?"

No one had an answer.

"What do you think?" Sam asked him.

"I think they shrink back down in size and hide. Maybe they sleep during the day and hunt at night."

"I've wondered, where did they come from?" Jonathan asked.

"No idea," Sam said.

"Aliens. I think they're from aliens," Spencer said behind them.

"It's as good of an explanation as I can come up with," Sam said.

"I found one," John called out. He placed it in the same bag.

They turned a corner in the path and came face-to-face with a large black bear. It was mating season and bears were on the hunt for mates. They all stopped and watched as the bear stared at them.

"What's going on?" Spencer said behind them. He walked up to where they stood and yelled out, "That's a bear!"

The bear stood up on his rear legs and growled. The pups barked but took cover behind their owners. Sam pointed his rifle at the bear and slid off the safety. If the bear charged, he was ready to kill it. But the bear relented and turned into the trees and left. The pups then barked louder and acted like they wanted to chase it.

"You guys are brave now," Orlando said.

"I think I peed my pants," Spencer said.

We looked down to see a big wet spot going down his shorts.

"I thought I might crap myself," Jonathan said, trying to relieve Spencer's embarrassment.

"You aren't the first person to do that when facing a bear that big," Sam said, feeling a bit sorry for Spencer.

"How do you think that bear would do against the monster?" Orlando asked.

Sam said, "The bear would rip it apart."

"I agree," John added.

They continued the walk but being more watchful off the trail for the bear's return.

They ended up finding five of the oblong objects by the time they got back to the pool. Storm found one of them.

"We'll take these to the police station and the others from the freezer to the funeral home," John said.

"Thank you, boys, for the help. You had better go home and change, Spencer," Sam said.

"I'm taking a shower and going back to bed," Spencer answered.

Orlando thought about asking if he could go with them but decided not to. He hadn't asked his mom and hated to leave the community without her permission. Instead, he went home and called August while Storm, who was pooped out, took a much-needed nap.

"Want to go to the pool?" he asked her.

"Sure. Now?"

"Yeah. I'll bring a cooler with some sodas."

"Okay. I'll bring April if you'll bring Jonathan."

"I'll call him."

"Please don't bring Spencer."

"He's sleeping anyway. See you there in a few."

He hung up and called Jonathan. He didn't tell him August was bringing April.

*In all* that had gone on last night and that morning, John and Sam forgot that they still were supposed to search Elm Street because the posse had run out of daylight the day before. There were three of the objects that had been dropped there a couple of days earlier and they would be opening on their own soon if they weren't destroyed.

Sam McGill and John Dunbar walked into the police station and asked for Chief Johanson.

"He's busy," the clerk told them.

"It's about the murder last night," John told the guy.

He left and then came back. "He has a little time. This way."

He led the two men back to the chief's office. Chief Johanson was sitting behind a large desk with a pile of papers a foot tall in front of him. John placed the plastic ziplock bag in front of him and they took seats in front of the desk.

"What is this?" the chief asked, pointing to the bag.

Sam began, “We know it’s hard to believe in the monsters we’ve told you about.”

“You think?” the chief said.

“These will prove it to you.”

“How will a few nuts prove it to me? You guys must be nuts.”

“Open them and you’ll see,” Sam told him.

“Explain.”

“Inside the shell is a monster. I opened one these Saturday evening and let the first monster out.”

“A monster is inside this shell?”

“It’s very small, but it grows very fast when released. We can’t explain it. We have no idea where it came from, but we keep finding these in yards and on trails throughout the woods around our community,” Sam told him.

“We believe Rufus opened some of these and was killed by them. I’ve seen them and I don’t want to see them again,” John said.

“The only way you’ll believe us is to open these. But be ready to kill the creatures as soon as you see them,” Sam said.

“And how do I do that?” the chief asked.

“Smash them, drown them, shoot them, whatever it takes,” Sam said.

Sam got up, and John followed his lead.

“Where are you going?” Chief Johanson asked.

“We have more of these to get rid of,” John told him.

Before they turned to leave the nutshells in the bags began moving back and forth.

“I would suggest you open them soon, or they’ll do it for you, and you don’t want that,” Sam McGill said.

The two men left the office. Chief Johanson sat there and stared at the bag as it rolled around his desk.

**Once** they were back in John's car, John said, "Let's hope the chief takes our advice."

**Orlando and Jonathan** found four chairs together and then went for a dip while they waited for August to arrive. Jonathan came up out of the water and saw August walk in with April. "She brought April," he smiled.

"Really?"

"As if you didn't know."

"I'm as surprised as you are," Orlando said smiling as he climbed out of the pool.

"We have lounge chairs over here!" he yelled out to them.

August was wearing a small light blue bikini. April had on a green flowered bikini. They both looked great. Orlando noticed that Rhonda Lewis was watching the girls as they walked by.

The girls smiled and waved.

"Thanks for saving us seats, Jonathan," April said to him.

"No problem," he said, as he noticed how April was smiling at him. Jonathan had never had a girlfriend either, and had never really thought about it. Having a girlfriend meant having to spend time with her instead of his two best buddies. He figured playing ball in the backyard was more fun than a girl. But, looking into April's eyes, his opinion might be changing.

He quickly laid down on his lounger. The two girls were lying on the two middle lounges with the boys next to them.

"Did you hear what happened last night?" Orlando asked the girls.

**Meanwhile,** in the police station, Chief Johanson called for one of his deputies to come to his office. The deputy walked in, and the chief told him to take the bag downstairs to the lab, a place where the policemen looked over evidence. The deputy looked at the bag as it moved around on the table.

"Are those Mexican jumping beans in the bag?" he asked.

"Of course not. Do they look like Mexican jumping beans?"

"I've never seen Mexican jumping beans, Chief. What do you want me to do with them down there?"

"Just keep an eye on them until I get there," he said.

The deputy picked the bag up carefully with two fingers and lifted it. The bag wriggled as he held it. He looked at the chief and left.

Chief Johanson went down the hall and found two of his best officers who were drinking coffee and eating donuts in the breakroom.

"Come with me," he ordered.

As he was leading the two men down the stairs he heard screaming from the lab. The three men began running toward the screams. They opened the door and ran to the officer who was looking down at the plastic bag. All five shells had burst open and five smiling faces were looking up at the officers through the plastic.

"What the hell are those?!" one of the officers yelled.

"I don't know," the chief said. The worm-like objects grew inside the bag as they stood there staring at them. They were pressing against the bag trying to get out. Then one of them had tiny arms pop out from under its body and began clawing at the plastic.

"Kill them!" Chief Johanson shouted.

One of the officers panicked and pulled his pistol and began shooting at the bag. The bullets bouncing off the metal table and into the walls.

One bullet hit the plastic bag and it popped open and the creatures crawled out.

"Stop shooting, Idiot," the chief yelled. By then most of the officers in the building were rushing down to the room to see where the shots were coming from. The chief picked up a heavy bound manual from the top of a cabinet and tried to smash the tiny monsters. Before the book could hit the table, the monsters moved off to the side and grew larger. They smiled and then reached for the officers. Soon two more men drew their guns and began firing. Two of the monsters fell but the other three slid off the table and under it.

"Where did they go?!"

"Under the table!"

"Get them!"

"How?!"

The men surrounded the table and lowered themselves to the floor. One of the creatures made a run toward one of the officers and jumped onto his face. He screamed and the creature grabbed his tongue with his T-Rex arms and pulled.

Another officer pulled out his Billy club and swung it hitting the thing, breaking the officer's nose in the process. The monster fell to the ground and the officer continued hitting it until it had died. That freaked out all the other officers and they began backing away from the table.

The two creatures that were still alive continued to grow bigger and soon had to come out from under the table. They grinned at the officers as they grew. Their eyes popped out of their heads and stared before making their attack. Every officer began shooting at the creatures. Once they were shot, it seemed as though the monsters deflated and fell to the floor in a heap, shrinking. One eyeball blinked, before closing for good.

**"You want me** to cremate these nuts?" the funeral director asked again.

"Martin, they aren't nuts. Believe me when I tell you this. There are monsters inside those shells," Sam McGill told him.

"Okay, sure. Are you okay?"

Sam had known Martin, the funeral director, for years. Sam had brought many loved ones to this same funeral home over the years. His parents, Patsy's parents, and a brother.

"Well, I don't believe it. But let's fire it up," Martin said.

Martin led the men downstairs to the crematorium; he fired up the cremator and placed the bag of shells inside. As they waited for the process to finish, they heard screams from inside the cremator. They were faint, but still heard. Martin looked at the two men with questioning eyes. Sam told him, "You wouldn't believe it. You probably don't want to know."

The screaming stopped, and it wasn't long before the process was done. "Would you like to pick up the remains later?" Martin asked.

"Can you dispose of them?" John asked.

"Of course."

"What do we owe you?"

"Nothing. Come back and visit."

"Hopefully, no time soon," Sam told him.

"I meant while you're still breathing," Martin said. The men laughed.

*"What were those, Chief?!"* one of the officers asked as they looked down at the monsters.

"I don't know. But those men were telling us the truth."

"What do we do?"

"I'm not sure, but that community is in grave danger. I was never taught how to fight monsters," Chief Johanson said.

# Chapter 12

**Orlando,** Jonathan, and the girls spent time in the water, had chicken fights, bought snacks and talked. They were having a great time until Spencer yelled out, "Where have you guys been? I've been looking everywhere for you."

The smiles that had been on the girls' faces turned into frowns as Spencer approached.

"Why didn't you call me?"

"You went back to bed. Remember?" Orlando reminded him.

"Oh, yeah," Spencer said.

"You girls look great. I really like your bikinis," Spencer told them, eyeing them from chest to toes.

He then turned and said, "I'm going for a snack."

"Too bad the monster didn't get Spencer," April said as soon as Spencer was out of hearing.

"That's a bit harsh," Orlando said.

"I don't actually mean it. He creeps me out. Did you see the way he stared at us?" April said.

"He definitely doesn't try to hide it," Jonathan said.

They watched Spencer as he walked to the concession stand, buy his snacks and swing by the lifeguard stand where Rhonda Lewis was sitting.

He stood there looking up at her while eating a Babe Ruth bar.

"What do you want, Spencer?" Rhonda asked him, irritated at his staring.

"I'm just admiring your legs," he told her. She kicked her leg out at him and hit his hand. The candy bar flew into the pool where some young kids were playing tag. One of the kids turned around to get away when he saw the bar floating in the pool.

He yelled out, "We have a floaty! Someone pooped in the pool!"

"Gross!"

"Get me out of here!"

"Who did it?!"

The kids were splashing and causing a ruckus as they were trying to leave the pool. One kid was making waves trying to get the turd away from him.

Spencer looked up at Rhonda and said, "Look what you did."

He jumped in the pool and grabbed the turd looking candy bar and took a bite.

A nine-year-old girl named Savannah yelled out, "That weirdo just ate the turd!"

Her sister, Shelby, yelled, "It's that gross boy!"

Spencer held the bar up in the air and shouted, "It's just a Babe Ruth bar!" He took another big bite.

April and August couldn't believe what Spencer was doing. Orlando and Jonathan believed it. They had seen things like this over and over from Spence. They even laughed.

"That's disgusting," April said.

"Plus, it had chlorine all over it," August said.

"He's not going to let a candy bar go to waste," Orlando told them.

"I once saw him reach into a urinal and pull out a dime," Jonathan said.

"Is he mental?" April asked.

"Maybe," Jonathan said.

"His parents had him tested," Orlando said.

"What were the results?" April asked.

"They would never say," Orlando said and laughed.

At that moment, Spencer walked up and took a seat on the lounge chair with April.

"Get off my chair," she said as she tried pushing him off with her feet.

"Want a bite?" he said. Offering her a bite of his candy bar.

Orlando figured Spencer must really like April, the boys had never seen Spencer share his treats. Even a treat that looked like a turd with chlorine on it.

"Gross, get that thing away from me," April said.

"Okay," he said as he continued eating it.

"I think it's time to go. I'm getting too much sun," April said.

She and August stood up, each of them wrapping their towels around their waist.

Orlando and Jonathan stood up.

"I guess it's time to go," Orlando said.

"But I just got here," Spencer said.

"You can stay and play with your young friends," Jonathan said.

"Or ask Rhonda to be your girlfriend again. Wear her down," Orlando said.

"I'm coming with you," Spencer said. As they all walked past Rhonda Lewis, Spencer winked at her and said, "Call me later."

"In your dreams," Rhonda said.

"Every night," he told her.

"Sicko," she said.

August gave Orlando a quick kiss on his cheek, and the two girls set off for their houses.

Orlando said, "Let's go to my house and play video games."

The three boys jumped on their bikes and took off.

I'll be there in a little bit. "I probably need to let Laddie out."

"Bring him over and he can play with Storm."

"Okay."

*Spencer* went straight to the fridge as soon as they entered the house.

"What have you got that's good?" he asked.

"Nothing for you. We have a hard enough time feeding ourselves. We aren't going to feed you."

"Can I have a Coke?"

"Sure."

He came back into the living room with the Coke and a big bag of chips. There was no use saying anything.

Jonathan arrived with Laddie. The two dogs sniffed each other and then curled up together on Storm's dog bed.

"The police are storming the neighborhood. Police cars are everywhere," Jonathan said. Orlando went to the windows and watched policemen as they walked between houses like they were searching for something.

"You think they're looking for the monsters or the killer?" Jonathan said.

"What killer?" Spencer asked.

"Did you not hear that a man and his dog were killed last night over on Elm Street?" Orlando said.

"Who was it?"

"A guy named Sean Bridges."

"Did the creatures get him?"

"We think so."

Orlando saw one of the patrolmen come up his driveway. He went to the door and opened it before he knocked.

"We're asking everyone in the community if they have had any encounters with any strange beings in the last couple of days," the cop said.

"Come on in," Orlando told him.

They went to the kitchen table and the four of them took seats. Then Orlando remembered to offer the officer a drink.

"Water would be great."

Orlando went to the dispenser and filled a glass with ice and water and sat it in front of the officer.

"We've got a story for you," Orlando told him.

The three boys spent the next hour telling him about their encounters. They told him about first being chased down the street on Saturday. They told about how the creature had crawled down the chimney and into the house. They told him every detail that they could remember. At times, all three of them were talking.

The cop was trying to take notes but was having trouble keeping up with them.

Orlando told him his theory of why they never see them during the day except for that first day when it was first released from the shell.

"I'm guessing that's why you have your fireplace plugged up with pillows?"

"Yes, sir. Mom had made us take them down the first day, but then the creature came in and attacked us. She made us put them back after that," Orlando told him.

"Anything else?" he asked.

"They're the scariest things in the world," Spencer told him.

"We know. We encountered them this morning. We believe you," he said. He wrote down our names, phone numbers, and addresses.

"You boys be careful. We're going to do our best to rid the community of these things."

"Thank you, Officer," Orlando said. The cop turned and left.

The three boys took turns playing video games until Spencer and Jonathan had to go home for supper.

Once Jonathan got home, his mother asked what Orlando was doing for supper.

"I don't know."

"Call and invite him to come eat with us," Jill said.

Orlando happily took them up on the offer and hurried over to their house, leaving Storm at home.

**Once** they were seated at the dinner table, Jonathan's father said a prayer and then they served the fried chicken, mashed potatoes and trimmings.

"The police came by today and asked if we had encountered anything strange. I told them no," Jill said. "It was so out of the blue."

Orlando looked at Jonathan. He knew that Jonathan's parents hadn't come to the meeting about the monsters. Apparently, he had never even told them about the monsters either.

"It must have been about Mr. Bridges dying last night," Mr. Miller said.

"What?" Jill asked her husband.

"I heard a tidbit about a man dying last night over on Elm Street," he said.

"That's awful. How?"

"Don't know."

After eating, Orlando motioned Jonathan to take him to his room. Once the door was closed Orlando said, "You haven't told your parents about the creatures?"

"No. I know how they are. If I told them, they would confine me and my brother and sister to the inside the house for the entire summer."

"But they need to know. What if they go outside for something after dark? You don't want to live with that if you could have warned them."

"I hadn't thought of that."

"I'll help you tell them."

"Okay," Jonathan said.

The two boys went downstairs and told his mom that the two of them needed to talk to her and his dad.

"What about?"

"Just wait until the two of you are here, please."

She could see the seriousness in his eyes. She left to go get her husband.

They came back into the dining room and took seats with the boys at the table.

"Okay, what's so important?" his father asked.

"This is going to be hard to believe, and I should have told you before now, but here goes…"

Jonathan told his parents pretty much the same story they had told the policeman. His parents kept quiet except for a few times. His mother would gasp from time to time. His father looked on, unconvinced. Jonathan's sister and brother walked in, and Jill sent them to their rooms.

"And this is what killed Rufus Langley and Mr. Bridges," Jill said after listening.

"Yes," Orlando said. "That's what the meeting was about last night. The police have encountered them too. That is why they were going around the neighborhood asking if anyone had encountered anything strange."

"The creatures only come out at night. We're okay during daylight."

"This is hard to believe, boys," Mr. Miller said.

"Call my mom when she gets home. Call John Dunbar or Sam McGill. They all have seen them," Orlando said.

"Why didn't you tell us about them before them?"

"I know how you worry. But Orlando convinced me that I needed to tell you. I don't want you guys going out at night with them roaming the neighborhood."

Jonathan got up to leave. His mother rose and hugged him. The two boys left for Jonathan's room.

Once they were gone, Mr. Miller went to the phone and called John Dunbar.

Ten minutes later, Jill's husband said, "He confirmed everything they told us. I guess we should have gone to the meeting."

"Maybe it's a good time to take a vacation," Jill said. "We could go to visit Mom in Florida. Maybe take the kids to Disneyland."

"I have to give my work notice. I can't just go when I want to."

"You can ask. It's not safe here," Jill said.

"John said that if we stay inside the house at night, we'll be safe. Don't let Laddie out after dark," he told Jill. "He said the police are now taking this seriously."

It was getting dark, and Orlando knew he needed to leave. He surrendered his video game.

"I've got to get home. It's almost dark," he said.

He hurried down the stairs and outside to his bike. Jonathan's home was only a few houses from his, but it was still risky in that short distance. He looked behind him as he rode his bike. He heard growling in the woods behind one of the houses. His nerves were about shot by the time he got home. He left the bike in the yard and punched the code into the keyless lock. The door unlocked and he rushed through.

Orlando knew his mom should be getting home soon after a long day at two jobs. He appreciated how hard she worked to take care of the two of them. He felt that his mom was an attractive woman and thought she should date. It would make her life a lot easier if she found a husband.

"When do I have time or energy to date?" she told him after he had suggested it. "Plus, someone would have to ask me out. I'm not doing a dating app."

"You could be the bachelorette on that TV show. You would have your pick of twenty men."

"They don't pick middle-aged women with a teenaged son," she said and laughed.

"They should. You would be great," he had told her. She hugged and kissed him.

He heard the garage door opening and ran to meet her. Once she had the car inside, he hit the button to close it. He wasn't taking any chances.

"Hi, honey. How was your day?" she asked after getting out of the twelve-year-old Toyota.

"Good. The police made a canvas today. They finally believe us about the monsters."

"I saw police vehicles on every street when I drove in. I wondered what was happening. There was a flyer on our mailbox."

"I didn't see it. They must be out searching for the creatures," Orlando said.

"Did you eat?"

"Mrs. Miller invited me to eat with them," Orlando told her.

"That was nice of her."

"Wait till I tell you what Spencer did at the pool today."

"Follow me upstairs and tell me. I need to hop in the shower."

# Chapter 13

**The police** were searching the neighborhood after dark. They went in pairs and held their guns in one hand. One officer had bear spray in his other hand and the other carried a flashlight. None of the officers were thrilled with the idea after many of them had seen the creatures earlier at the station. Each officer had a radio attached to their vest.

Chief Johanson sat in John Dunbar's kitchen and controlled everything from there. He knew they were at such a disadvantage. They didn't know what size the creatures would be since they changed sizes. They had no idea how many there were. Were there more of the oval shaped shells out there hatching as they searched? The Chief was determined to have his men spend the night searching for the creatures.

**The three creatures** were on the move. They could sense that something was different. They moved together to the back of a house on Oak Street. The house stood at the very end of the cul-de-sac, four houses west of Sam McGill's home. They saw a light beam shining in the side yard and lighting up the trees in the woods.

They climbed the outside brick and positioned themselves just around the corner. A position where they could ambush the policemen.

"Any activity yet? Over," the chief asked.

"Nothing so far. Over," one of the officers responded. The Chief had six officers. They were out there searching in groups of two.

The chief had given each group a number, 1, 2 and 3.

"Check in. Group one."

“Okay,” came the agreed upon response.

“Group two.”

“Okay.”

“Group three.”

“Okay.”

The two officers knew better than to walk around a corner too close to the building. That was where the most danger was when doing a search. They swung out between the houses and moved into the backyard while not knowing that the three creatures were attached to the rear of the house.

One officer shined his light on the trees in the woods and then swung it around to the back of the house. Once the light was near them, the three monsters attacked. They moved fast toward the officers only thinking of liver. The two officers panicked and began shooting uncontrollably. One of the officers hit one of the monsters and it went down in a heap. The other two creatures then shrunk in size and escaped around the side of the house as the officers chased them shooting. They slithered up the front of the house and over the roof and back down the other side and into the backyard again. They rushed back into the woods.

The officers never saw them again.

“I heard shots,” said the chief over the radios.

The officer in group three announced, “We were attacked on Oak Street. Killed one. The other two escaped.”

“All officers go to Oak Street. I’m on my way,” the chief directed.

Bill and Helen opened their front door and looked at the two officers who were standing in their front yard.

“What is happening out here?!” Bill asked angrily.

The next morning, they would discover ten bullet holes in the side and back of the house. One through a downspout. Two through windows. One in the back door and six in the brick.

The two creatures continued their hunting that night in the woods. They killed and ate the livers of two opossums, a deer, and a racoon. But they wanted human liver.

**Francine** had the morning off. She didn't have to be at work until noon. She got up and fixed French toast for herself and Orlando. They talked, while eating, about the police search and what he was up to yesterday.

He told her about asking August to be his girlfriend. He never kept secrets from his mother.

"I like August. She seems like a sweet girl. But I don't want her here at the house alone with you. You understand?"

"Mom, we wouldn't. You told me already."

"I know, but I'm sure her mother would feel the same," Francine told him.

"Okay."

"If you have other friends with you, it's okay for her to be here," Francine said.

He then told her about Spencer, asking Rhonda Lewis to be his girlfriend.

"I know that didn't go over very well," Francine said.

"Not at all."

The conversation turned back to the creatures. "I wonder if they killed any of the monsters last night," Orlando said.

"Sam might know," his mother offered. "Where do you think they came from?"

"Spencer thinks they came from aliens," Orlando told her.

"You're talking about UFO's?"

"Yeah. I mean it's the most logical explanation. Where else would a new species come from? Unless a caterpillar was dumped in some chemical and it changed its composition. You know, like a boy getting bit by a spider and turning into Spiderman."

“But that’s fantasy, this is real,” his mother said.

“I know, that’s what’s so crazy about it. If I wrote and illustrated a comic about these creatures, everyone would think it was fantasy.”

Storm padded into the kitchen and sat on the floor next to Orlando looking for a handout. Orlando cut off a piece of his French toast and dipped it in syrup and gave it to him. Storm woofed it down and then continued licking his lips.

“You shouldn’t do that. He’ll expect it all the time,” Francine said as she got up to place her plate in the dishwasher.

Orlando got up and did the same and then took Storm outside, so he could run around the back yard. Francine walked out and took a seat on the patio and watched them play. She was happy to see how much they enjoyed each other. The June sunshine felt good against her face and legs.

Francine heard the phone ring and got up to answer it.

“Hello.”

“This is Sam McGill. Is Orlando there?”

“Yes. But first, do you know if the police got any of the creatures last night?"

“I was told they killed one, but two escaped.”

“There’s two more?”

“That they know of. We’re doing another yard sweep today looking for the nut-like shells. We would like for the boys to help.”

“I’ll get Orlando for you,” she said.

Many of the residents that could come met at the meeting house at ten that morning. Francine went with Orlando to help till she had to leave for work. Jonathan, Spencer, August and April were there. There were maybe another twenty people there to help. John Dunbar quickly explained to everyone what they were going to do.

He passed around sheets of paper showing a picture of the shells they were looking for.

"I'm going to place these on every mailbox asking people to check their yards every day. If you find any, they must be brought to either me or Sam McGill. Do not keep these in your house under any circumstances. We will destroy them."

John split everyone into two groups. Orlando and his friends, his mother, and others went with Sam. The others went with John.

Sam's group went to Elm Street while John's crew went to Ash Street and started the search.

Spencer said, "I was hoping we would be going down Ash Street. I wanted to see my girlfriend."

August told him, "Rhonda Lewis is not your girlfriend and never will be."

"That's hurtful," he said.

"The sooner you accept it the better it will be for you," August told him.

"I'd rather be eaten by the creatures," Spencer said.

"We can arrange that," Jonathan said, as the others laughed.

They spread three feet apart and began the search. Orlando noticed a man he figured to be around his mother's age, and he didn't have a ring on his finger. He was a pleasant looking man that he had never seen before.

"Hey, August, do you know who that guy is?"

He motioned toward the guy. "Yeah. He just moved into the neighborhood about a month ago."

"Where?"

"In the house next to April. His name is ...uh...Lucas something," she answered.

"Is he married?"

"No. He lives there alone. Why?"

"Nothing. I've just never seen him before."

"Found one!" a lady called out. Sam walked over to her and she held out a walnut in her hand.

"That is an old walnut," Sam told her. He unfolded his paper and showed it to her, "See how this is round, but the one in the picture is oval shaped."

"Oh, yes, I remember now. Sorry."

"That's okay. Don't be afraid to question things."

She placed the walnut in her pocket.

Later that morning she found what she thought was another one and stuck it in her pocket with the other one. She loved walnuts.

"Here's one," Orlando called out. He walked over and handed it to Sam, who placed it in his plastic bag.

After they had searched Elm Street, they were standing around talking before moving on when Orlando took the opportunity to introduce his mother to Lucas.

He walked her over to him and said, "I wanted to introduce ourselves to you."

Lucas smiled and said, "That's awfully neighborly. I'm Lucas West."

He held out his hand for Orlando and Francine to shake. Lucas was around six foot tall, slim, with dark hair that had a tint of grey around the temples. Orlando figured his mom would think he was handsome.

"I'm Orlando and this is my mother, Francine Gomez."

"Glad to meet you," Francine said

"My pleasure," he told her, while looking into her eyes.

Orlando thought he could see his mother's knees go weak as she smiled at him.

"Have you lived here long?" she asked.

"Moved to Ash Street about a month ago."

"Where from?"

"An apartment in town. Wanted to be in a community. Some grass to cut. Love it here, except for the monster thing," he smiled, with perfect white teeth.

After searching Elm Street, they continued down the east side of Maple Street and then onto Oak Street as Francine and Lucas talked.

Francine looked at her phone and then up at Lucas and said, "I'm running late. I need to go get ready for work. It was nice meeting you."

"I'll see you later." Orlando could tell that Lucas was disappointed that his mom had to leave.

"Orlando, I have to leave. Be careful. I'll be home around eight-thirty."

"Okay, Mom. Love you."

"Love you more."

The team continued the search and found two shells in Ruth Johnson's yard. By the time the two teams had searched the entire neighborhood they had a total of eleven oblong shells in the two bags.

The lady, Peggy Whitt, who had placed what she thought were two walnuts in her pocket, went to her home on Elm Street and placed them on her counter and went to her easy chair and took a nap. Peggy's husband worked for the local electric company and wouldn't be home 'til later. Their children were grown and out of the house. The one shell she had assumed was also a walnut began to move on her counter.

*The three boys* went back to Orlando's house. Orlando took Storm outside to run for a bit. The dog went to the edge of the woods and sniffed around. He came back with something in his mouth. Orlando told him to drop it. The pup obeyed, and out dropped an oval shaped shell.

"That's one of those shells!" Spencer cried out.

"It sure is."

"What are you going to do with it?" Jonathan asked Orlando.

"I'm not keeping it. We'll take it to Sam."

"Hey. Storm found it over there by the edge of the woods. There may be others," Spencer said.

They ran over to the tree line and searched. Storm was there sniffing again. Five minutes later, Storm ran up to Orlando and dropped another shell at his feet. The shepherd seemed to have monster sniffing ability.

After searching for another ten minutes with no other results, the boys headed back into the house. Orlando locked the house up and took off for Sam's house. Storm walked with them.

Orlando rang the doorbell, and a few seconds later Patsy McGill answered the door.

"Hi, boys. What can I do for you?"

"Is Sam home?" Orlando asked.

"No. He left with John Dunbar."

"Does he have a cell phone with him?"

"No. He never wanted one. He says they're a headache."

"Would you have him call me when he gets back home?" Orlando asked.

"Sure. Is there something I can help you with?"

"No. It's to do with monsters."

"Okay. You boys be careful," Patsy told them before closing the door and locking it.

The community had always been so safe. People usually never locked their doors during the day. But things had changed during the past few days. Most of the community was made up of young families with a sprinkling of older retired folks. In the summer, you would see kids out playing in their yards, running through sprinklers, and playing games. Today, Orlando didn't see a single child out in the yard as they walked back to his house.

"I'm going to go home for lunch," Spencer said.

"See ya, Spence."

"What do you want to do?" Jonathan asked.

"We could invite the girls over to play games," Orlando suggested.

"You mean August and April?"

Orlando nodded. "Okay," Jonathan said.

Orlando called August and invited her and April to come over. April was at her house, and they said they would be there soon.

"Are you going to ask April to be your girlfriend?" Orlando said.

"I don't know. I like her and everything, but do I really want to be tied down to one girl?"

"Okay, Romeo. I haven't seen a line of girls at your door. I can tell she likes you."

Jonathan shrugged. Orlando went to get some snacks to put out and went to his room to get some games they could play.

While the girls were riding over they talked about what Orlando said when he invited them over.

"He said games. He invited us over to play games."

"What kind of games? Maybe post office, or spin-the-bottle, or seven minutes in heaven," April said.

"What is seven minutes in Heaven?" August asked.

"A boy and a girl are picked, and they go together in a dark closet, and they can do whatever they want. Usually, a lot of kissing and maybe groping."

"What if you don't like the boy?"

"You don't have to do anything. You can just talk," April told her.

"How do you know this stuff?"

"Haven't you been to a teenage party?"

"No. And I don't think that's the kinds of games Orlando meant."

April's body was more mature than August's was. August wore a bra but didn't really need one. April had been wearing one for two years. A lot of teenage boys thought she was much older than she was.

After Jonathan opened the door, the girls crouched down and petted Storm and then Jonathan led them to the kitchen table where they saw the games and snacks.

"Board games?" April said, as she looked at the table.

"You guys can pick whichever game you like," Orlando said, not noticing her disappointment.

He had Pictionary, Careers, Monopoly, Risk and Sequence on the table, plus a deck of cards.

"Sequence would be fun," August said.

"I don't know that game," April said.

"It's simple and we can play teams. Guys against the girls," August said.

Orlando spread the game on the table and explained the rules to April.

"What would you two want to drink?"

He got up and poured drinks into glasses and passed them out. He placed the snacks around the table.

As they began the game, Orlando said, "Storm found two more shells in the back yard."

"What did you do with them?" August asked.

"Actually, they're still in my pocket."

He reached into his pocket and placed them on the table. They all stared at the shells.

"It's so strange thinking about there being a monster inside each one," August said.

"I know. Hopefully you'll never see one," Jonathan said.

"What are you going to do with them?" April asked.

"We tried to give them to Mr. McGill, but he was already gone. He's supposed to call be when he gets back."

They continued the game taking turns placing tokens trying to make a sequence of five in a row.

Halfway through the game one of the shells began wobbling on the table.

**Peggy Whitt** woke up and went to the bathroom. One of the two shells on the counter had cracked open and a worm-sized monster crawled out of the shell. It doubled in size almost as soon as it was out. It walked across the counter and down the kitchen cabinets to the floor, doubling in size again as it walked, leaving slime behind. The thing heard the toilet flush and headed for the hallway. The monster doubled and then doubled again in size. It was now almost four feet long. The creature walked down the hall until the door opened and the lady walked out.

She sensed something in the hall and looked up at the creature. Its eye popped out as the creature extended it to within three feet of the woman. She screamed and rushed back into the guest bathroom and slammed the door and locked it before the monster could get her.

The monster pushed on the door with its T-Rex arms with no luck. Peggy looked for a weapon in case the door was knocked down. The only thing she could find was the toilet plunger. Her husband liked keeping it handy.

The creature had no luck pushing on the door. It then shrunk back down to the worm size it had been. It easily crawled under the door and into the bathroom. Peggy was panicking. She was looking for something else to use in the medicine cabinet and dropped a medicine bottle onto the floor. She looked down and saw the monster enter under the door.

The monster looked up at her and smiled. She took the plunger and plunged it over the top of the creature and began plunging the crap out of it, up and down, up and down, up and down.

'How would I know if I killed it?' she thought to herself.

She plunged again and again and again. She left the plunger stuck to the floor. She was afraid of removing it in case the monster hadn't died. Her problem was she couldn't open the door with the plunger stuck to the floor. It was in the way.

She sat on the toilet and waited for her husband to come home. She had a three hour wait.

# Chapter 14

**April yelled out,** "That thing is moving!"

The four of them stared at the shell as it shook.

"You have to do something!" August shouted.

Orlando wasn't sure what to do. He looked for something to smash it with, and then he saw the microwave oven. He picked up the two shells and placed them in the oven and closed the door.

The shell cracked open just as Orlando closed the door. He punched in five minutes and the microwave began heating. The creature's eye came flush against the glass, and it smiled. Then the thing screamed. It was a muffled scream. The four teenagers stood watching in horror as they watched the creature shrivel up and die. The other shell popped open like popcorn, and the second creature screamed before also dying.

And then their eyes popped covering the glass in a grey slimey substance.

The four of them screamed and the girls jumped into the arms of the two boys. While being held by Jonathan, April grabbed his head and pulled it down to where she gave him a big kiss. For a moment, Jonathan forgot what they had just witnessed.

"Wait, you thought this was a good time for a kiss?" Jonathan said.

"Why not?" she asked. "It might be our last chance."

He let go of her, ignored her question, and asked Orlando, "I guess we need to clean up that mess?"

"I'm going to let them cook a while longer," Orlando said.

The phone rang causing August to jump. Orlando answered.

"This is Sam. Patsy said you called."

"I did, but we took care of it. Storm found two more shells."

"How did you take care of them?"

“We microwaved them,” Orlando told him.

Sam began laughing. Orlando listened to him laugh until he stopped. Sam then said, “I don’t guess that’s much different than what we’re doing with them.”

“Storm seems to have a nose for finding them,” Orlando told him.

“Let’s take him out on the trails in the morning and let him hunt then,” Sam said.

“Okay. What time?”

“Meet you at the trail head at nine.”

“See you then, Mr. McGill. Bye.”

Orlando hung up and went over to look at the mess inside the microwave oven.

“How are we going to clean that up?” Jonathan asked.

“Here, let a woman take care of it,” April said.

Jonathan chuckled and said, “You’re a woman?”

“Closer than you,” she said.

There was a knock on the front door. Orlando left to answer it.

“It’s Spencer!” Orlando yelled.

“Don’t answer it!” April yelled out just after Orlando had opened the door.

“She doesn’t like you,” Orlando whispered to Spencer.

“Why not?”

Orlando shrugged.

Spencer walked into the kitchen and asked, “Why don’t you like me?”

“Do you want to know? Do you really, really, really want to know?”

“No. Not really,” Spencer said. “What are you guys doing?” he asked as he walked over to where April was starting to clean out the oven.

“What’s in there?”

Orlando answered, "Storm found two more shells and they started to open, so we nuked them."

"Cool! I miss all the fun."

"Maybe because you're not fun," April told him.

"Did you get up on the wrong side of the bed?" Spence asked.

April huffed as she removed a glob from the oven and dumped it into the garbage bag. Once she had gotten most of the goop out of the oven, she took Windex and sprayed it all around the inside and then took paper towels and wiped it down.

Orlando had to admit that it looked clean. He took the bag out to the garbage can.

When he came back inside, Spencer was telling April, "You're probably at that time of the month. That's why you're acting like a witch. It happens to my mom."

"Maybe it's because your mom had you," April fired back.

Orlando tried to be peacemaker, "Can't we just get along?"

"I think we better leave," August said. "It's getting close to supper time."

Orlando looked at the clock and saw that it was only three-thirty.

"Okay, see you tomorrow." August went over and hugged Orlando and kissed his cheek and left with April.

"Good. They're gone. Let's play video games," Spencer said.

The three boys went to the living room and turned on the Nintendo.

Spencer looked at Jonathan and asked, "Are you going to ask April to be your girlfriend?"

"Nope."

"How come?"

"I don't like the way she talks to you. You're my friend."

"Really?"

"I don't need a girlfriend, but I need my real friends," Jonathan explained.

Spencer jumped on him and started hugging and kissing him as they wrestled around the couch and then on the floor.

"I've changed my mind!" Jonathan yelled out.

*Three hours later*, Peggy Whitt was still stuck in the bathroom when she heard the front door open.

"Peggy!" her husband called out.

"Joe, I'm in here!" she yelled. He followed the sound.

"Where!" he called while standing in the hallway.

"I'm stuck in here," she said, hearing his voice close by.

"What do you mean, you're stuck? On the toilet?"

"I trapped one of the monsters. I may have killed it, but I can't open the door."

"What? Where? How?" He had a thousand questions forming in his mind.

"I stuck a plunger over it next to the door and can't lift it in case it's still alive."

"How do you trap a monster under a plunger?"

"Would you please just help me?"

"Okay. Open the bathroom window. I'll get the step ladder and climb in."

"Be careful dear." Peggy and Joe were in their late fifties and not the most physical of people. Joe was 5' 8" and two hundred and forty pounds.

He went to the garage and got the ladder and carried it around to the window. He climbed up to the opening and carefully crawled face first through the window with Peggy's help.

He stood up and looked at the plunger. "The monster couldn't have been very big."

"It was big when I first saw it. It was probably three to four feet long. I ran in here. A minute later in crawled under the door. It had shrunk. I placed the plunger over it and plunged a dozen times trying to kill it. I was afraid to take it off in case it wasn't dead."

Joe walked over to the plunger and started to lift it off. He hesitated, and then he plunged it another good dozen times. He lifted the plunger off the floor with a pop and looked down. Nothing was there.

"Are you sure you trapped it?"

"I'm positive."

He turned the plunger over to look inside it. The monster smiled at him and then its eye popped out toward him. He slammed the plunger back to the floor before it could escape. He plunged it further away from the door to where they could escape the bathroom. They closed the door behind them. Joe ran to the phone and called 911, and then called John Dunbar.

A few minutes later they heard sirens coming their way. They were standing in their front yard waiting for the police. Neighbors came out of their houses to see what the commotion was.

Joe quickly explained to the two officers what the problem was and where to go. One of the patrolmen called Chief Johanson. Neither of them was anxious to solve the problem. Betsy and Roger Williams, their neighbors, walked up to Peggy and Joe and asked, "What's going on?"

Peggy answered, "We have a monster trapped under a plunger and can't kill it."

"Okay, don't tell us," Betsy said as they walked away.

**Chief Johanson** arrived and was told about the problem.

"Do you have a flat shovel?" the chief asked Roger Williams.

"Yes."

"Why don't you get it for us?"

Roger went to his garden shed and retrieved the shovel and handed it to one of the policemen. The chief led two of his deputies into the bathroom and found the plunger stuck to the floor. He had one of the deputies fill the bathtub with water. The deputy was instructed to slide the shovel under the plunger.

"Be careful."

The deputy lifted the plunger to the side to unstick it and then slid the shovel under.

"Now place it in the water. We'll drown the thing," the chief said.

They had to tilt the shovel so they could get the air out of the plunger and have it fill with water. They then left the plunger in the water for at least ten minutes.

What they didn't know about the creature was that it had the ability to breathe underwater like a fish. The opening where the T-Rex arms came out of also acted as gills. The creature grew to its maximum possible size inside the plunger and waited to be released.

Finally Chief Johanson told the deputy to remove the shovel and the plunger. The three of them looked into the water to find the worm size creature. They saw it lying on the bottom of the tub. They couldn't figure out why the thing didn't float to the top.

As they stared at it, it began to grow bigger.

"Is it dead?" one of the deputies asked.

"It looks like it's bloating," another one said.

As they watched, the creature grew to a foot long.

"Is it dead?" he asked again.

"I don't think it's dead," the other cop said as he pulled out his pistol.

It looked up through the water and smiled, and then suddenly its eye popped out of the water, and it quickly climbed the bathtub toward the cops. The deputy began shooting at it. The bullets bounced around the bathroom off the metal tub. The chief dove out of the bathroom. The other deputy was hit by a stray bullet in his arm. Finally, a bullet hit its mark and the creature deflated and sunk back into the water.

Outside, a crowd had gathered. John Dunbar was trying to get details on what was going on. No one knew. They heard the shots ring out from inside the house. John figured another creature was involved.

Ten minutes later, Chief Johanson led his men out of the house. The one deputy had his arm in a sling made from a towel. Blood was soaking the white towel. The other deputy carried a bag with something in it. The crowd didn't know that it was one of the monsters, dead inside.

"What can you tell me, Chief?" John asked.

Chief Johanson ignored him and looked toward the Whitt's and said, "It's taken care of." The crowd grew more restless.

"We deserve to know what happened!" a woman called out.

"This is our neighborhood!"

"What are you doing about the monsters?!" a man yelled.

"He's doing nothing!" another one yelled.

"Time to call in the FBI!" The chief heard the shouts, especially the last one. The chief was a proud man, never wanting to admit his mistakes. He became chief because of his toughness. He didn't want the FBI or anyone else taking over his jurisdiction.

***The three boys*** rode up to the crowd on their bikes. They saw the police cruisers drive away. Peggy and Joe Whitt were telling their neighbors about the creature that was in their bathroom.

The crowd's attention turned to John Dunbar. They wanted answers. One of the men said, "You're the president of the community. You need to do something."

"I've been doing all I can. I can't force people to come to the meetings. I can't force people to search their yards for the shells, and I can't keep people from taking them into their houses!"

"Call for a mandatory meeting! Its past the time of being nonchalant about this!"

Orlando looked at his buddies and said, "The crowd is getting impatient."

"It's about time," Jonathan said.

They went over to where John was trying to answer everyone's questions. When the crowd finally dispersed, Orlando told him, "Why not call the FBI?"

"I would think Chief Johanson would have already done that," John told him.

"Maybe not. It wouldn't hurt."

John looked at the boys and said, "Okay. I'll go call."

"Can we come?"

"Sure," he said, although he really didn't want them to.

They went into his house and followed him into his den. He opened his computer and typed in, 'How to contact the FBI?'.

He found a customer service number and dialed it. A lady answered, "Hello, this is the FBI. How can I help you?"

"I need to talk to someone about monsters in our community."

She hung up on him.

"Maybe, don't mention monsters right off the bat," Orlando suggested.

John dialed the number again and put the cell phone on speaker.

"Hello, this is the FBI. How can I help you?"

"Could I talk to someone about a big problem in our community that I think the FBI would be interested in?"

"What problem would that be sir?"

"Aliens. You know, the UFO type," John told her.

"Have you seen them, sir?"

"Yes, they've invaded our community."

"Did you just call mentioning monsters?"

"Yes, but that's what I call them."

"Okay, let me transfer your call. Hold, please."

A minute later, a man came on the line and said, "This is the AARO. How can I help you?"

"I'm sorry. What is AARO?" John asked.

"The All-domain Anomaly Resolution Office. We are an office within the Secretary of Defense that investigates phenomena, including UFO's. Who am I talking to?"

"My name is John Dunbar, and I'm the president of our community association here in Minnesota."

"How can I help you, Mr. Dunbar."

"Okay, what we have is a bit unusual."

"Everything we deal with is a bit unusual," he said.

John went on and told the man about the shells and the creatures inside. He told him about the people and animals who had died and how the monster only took the livers of their victims.

"Who can vouch your story?"

"I have three teenagers here with me who have encountered them. The local police chief, Chief Johanson, has encountered and killed some of the monsters."

"Do you have any video of the monsters or creatures?"

"No. But our community is falling apart."

"Give me your full name, address, phone number, and social security number and we'll get back to you after I talk to my superiors."

John gave him the info he wanted and thanked him and hung up.

Ted looked up John Dunbar on their database to see if he had any red flags he should know about. He seemed clean.

"Do you think they'll do anything?" Spencer asked.

"I don't know. And who knows how long it might take for them to come here," Mr. Dunbar said.

# *Chapter 15*

***Ted Wilson*** had heard a lot of strange things during his time with AARO, but this one tops the cake. It was so strange, it made him believe it. Who could make up something that weird?

He knocked on his boss's doorframe and Charles Morton motioned him into his office.

"I just got a strange call from a man in Minnesota about creatures …" Ted went on to tell Charles what he had been told.

"Have you ever heard of anything like this?" Ted asked.

"No. But that's what makes it the more curious," Mark said.

"The man seemed sincere and at his wit's end."

"Do you want to go check it out and report back?" Mark asked Ted.

"Yes."

"Leave as soon as you can," Mark told him.

"Yes, Sir. Should I fly commercial or take a company plane?"

"I think commercial would be best."

Ted went back to his office and made a reservation for early the next morning. He called John Dunbar back and told him he would be arriving around noon the next day. John was very surprised.

***The boys were still*** there when John received the call-back. They were looking at John's collection of old vinyl albums. John had many of the bands from the 60's and 70's. He had all of The Beatles' albums.

Francine had introduced The Beatles to Orlando at an early age and he loved the songs and the different sounds they had mastered.

"I'm surprised, but he's coming tomorrow. Said he'd be here by noon," John told the boys. He dialed Sam McGill's number and told him about the call and the visitor.

Orlando led the boys out of John's house, and they rode their bikes back toward their houses. They stopped at Spencer's house. It was almost supper time. They stood there saying goodbye when Orlando said, "We need to film the creatures."

"What?" Spencer said.

"If we get film of them then the guy that's coming will have to believe us," Orlando said.

"Do you have a movie camera? I don't," Spencer said.

"Yes. My phone. It has video," Orlando said.

"And when are we going to get this video?" Spencer asked.

"Tonight, we must get it tonight. He's coming tomorrow."

"We should have filmed them in the microwave," Jonathan said.

"That would have been neat. Blamo! Guts everywhere!" Spencer said, trying to recreate the scene he hadn't seen.

"I've got to get home for dinner. I'll call you later," Jonathan said.

"Call me too. I don't want to miss it," Spencer said.

Orlando got home and took Storm out into the backyard. He was hoping the dog might find another shell. They had a small trail that led into the woods that the boys had cut over the years. Around a hundred yards inside was the clubhouse they had built. As they've gotten older, they've used it less and less. He walked down the trail toward it with Storm by his side. The woods were getting darker with each step. The sun was setting, and Orlando knew they needed to get back soon, but he wanted to see the clubhouse.

Two hundred feet to his left, the creatures were waking up and hungry. The liver they wanted wasn't eaten like other animals. The creatures absorbed the liver leaving no waste. Orlando reached into his pocket and noticed that he didn't have bear spray with him. He had forgotten to grab one. He decided to turn around and head home. Suddenly, Storm began barking at something further down the trail.

Orlando called out, “Storm! Storm! No! Come!”

The barking continued and Orlando ran down the path to where he found the dog face-to-face with a moose.

Orlando knew that moose were dangerous, even more dangerous than bears at times, especially the males with the huge antlers. If the moose charged it would be hard to get out of the way. Orlando reached down and picked up the pup and backed away, the pup continued its barking. The moose took a couple of steps toward them and then began grazing. Orlando hurried back to the safety of his yard.

His phone rang and he saw it was his mom. “Hi, Mom.”

“Have you eaten anything yet?”

“No.”

“I could bring home subs.”

“That sounds good.”

“You want your usual?”

“Sure.”

“Be home later,” she said and hung up.

Orlando took Storm back into the house. It was getting too dark to be outside. Orlando sat in his favorite chair and thought about how he could get a video of the monsters.

He knew it would be much too dangerous to creep around the neighborhood hoping to run into one of them after dark. The only idea that made sense was to find another shell or two and film the shell opening with the creature inside. He looked out the front window and saw Mr. Dunbar in front of his house posting a flyer on their mailbox.

He ran to the mailbox and grabbed it and ran back inside. He sat in his chair and read it.

It read:

Fellow neighbors of The Woods. As most of you should know by now, we have monsters roaming our neighborhood after dark. We've lost two of our friends to them so far, Rufus Langley and Sean Bridges.

We've also lost many of our dear pets that were in their yards after dark. I urge all of you to stay in your houses once it starts to get dark. If you find any shell-like oblong objects in or around your yard, please call me immediately. These shells contain monsters. Do not open them under any circumstances!!

I have called the Dept. of Defense, and they are sending a representative to investigate our claims. He will be here tomorrow. Stay safe.

President of the home association,

John Dunbar

He then listed his phone number.

Orlando reread the flyer again. He thought it explained the situation well.

Jonathan called and he answered.

"So, what's the plan?"

"I don't guess we can do anything until morning. It's too dangerous to go out tonight," Orlando told him. "Did you see the flyer yet?"

"What flyer?"

"John posted a flyer on everyone's mailbox."

"I see it hanging out there," Jonathan said, while looking out the window.

"What's the plan tomorrow?"

"I think we need to find a shell and open it. We can film the creature coming out."

"That sounds stupid," Jonathan said.

"We can put it in the microwave again and film it while it's inside. That way it's not dangerous," Orlando explained.

"Is your mom going to be there?"

"Let me check." He went to the blackboard and checked the schedule.

"She has a house to clean at eight in the morning and then she works at the grocery after that."

"I'll be there at eight. I'll call Spencer and tell him."

"He won't get up that early," Orlando said.

"I know. But he can't say we didn't tell him."

"Okay."

Orlando called August and told her his plans. He normally wouldn't have told her. But he wasn't sure what the correct thing was to do when you had a girlfriend. Were you supposed to include them in everything?

After telling her, he said, "Oh, there's a flyer on your mailbox."

"Dad already got it and read it to us. He told us that in no way were we to go outside for anything after seven-thirty."

"But it doesn't get dark till after eight-thirty."

"He wants us to be safe," she said.

"I wish everyone was like that," Orlando told her. They talked until he heard the garage door going up. He said goodbye, hung up and ran to the garage door and hit the button as soon as the car cleared the electronic eye.

Once his mom was inside the kitchen, he handed her the flyer and she read it.

"The guy is coming tomorrow, huh?" Francine said.

"We were with John when he called them."

"Wow."

Orlando went on to tell her about what had happened at the Whitt's house and how a cop had been shot.

"Who shot him?"

"Don't know. Must have been himself or another cop. The monster couldn't have done it."

"Something happens every day. And I thought this was a nice quiet neighborhood," she said.

"It's nicer with Lucas in it, huh?" Orlando said, teasing.

"He was very nice," she said as she started up the stairs to the shower. She stopped and said, "And not bad to look at."

They both laughed.

"You ought to ask him over for dinner," Orlando yelled out.

Francine didn't respond.

Orlando ate his sub while watching TV. They both went to bed early. Orlando thought about how to film the creature. The only safe way was to find a shell and nuke it in the microwave as he filmed it like they had earlier that day.

*While Orlando thought* about the monsters, two of them had awakened and begun their nightly hunt for liver. They began their hunt in Francine's backyard. They didn't realize that two of their urps had opened and the monsters were searching Elm Street for the same thing.

The urps had been deposited just off a trail in the woods where one of the creatures had eaten the liver of a opossum. The search posse had walked right past it.

The monsters went from yard to yard with no results. They searched for ways to get into houses where they realized the humans were. The fireplaces in the community had now all been blocked. They looked through windows and saw humans in front of TV's but couldn't get to them. It was frustrating. On Ash Street, the four creatures saw each other. There were no polite hellos. Not even a nod or blink of an eye to signal a sign.

They simply joined up and continued the hunt. They suddenly saw a door open, and a person came out onto the backyard patio.

Rhonda Lewis had the responsibility of checking to make sure people weren't sneaking into the pool area for a night swim. Folks had been known to go skinny dipping after dark - totally against community and pool rules. Since Rhonda's house backed up to the pool, she would come out to check it each night. She highly doubted anyone would be out due to the community mandate to stay inside after dark.

She thought she heard movement. She turned and saw four monsters rushing toward her. She screamed, turned and tripped over a raised patio paver, but kept her balance. The creatures were within five feet of her when she slammed the patio door shut and locked it. The creatures slammed into the door, each of their eyes staring at her. Their smiles turned to frowns.

Rhonda told herself, "From now on, I don't care if people want to skinny dip at night."

Rhonda's mom hurried into the room and asked, "What happened?"

Her mom could see the terror in her daughter's face.

"The monsters were in our backyard. They almost caught me," Rhonda said as tears fell down her cheeks. Her mom wrapped Rhonda in her arms and stared out the door but couldn't see anything.

"I'll call John Dunbar."

She released her daughter and picked up her cell phone and called John.

"Hello. This is John."

"This is Helen Lewis. The monsters were just in our backyard."

"Is everyone okay?"

"Yes. They almost got Rhonda. She went out on the patio to check the pool. She's quite shaken."

"Tell her to forget about the pool until we get rid of these creatures. And please stay in your house after dark." They hung up.

Rhonda went straight to bed and had nightmares.

Friday

***Just after midnight*** a young couple from town slipped into the pool to skinny dip. They stripped off their clothes and walked into the pool. They both were seventeen and were going to be seniors in Rhonda's class at high school. The couple had snuck into the pool before.

The four creatures heard the movement of the water and returned to Lewis's backyard. They saw the two humans in the pool. They were embraced. The monsters shrunk and went through the metal fencing and walked down the side of the pool at the opposite side of the couple.

The couple were too busy kissing and groping one another to see the growing monsters. The creatures walked on the bottom of the pool until they were only a few feet from the couple. The young couple's screams were not heard as the creatures pulled them under water until they drowned. The creatures then removed the livers and absorbed them underwater.

# *Chapter 16*

***Chief Johanson*** received a call Friday morning from Lisa Ramsey's mother, reporting her daughter missing.

"How long has she been missing, Mrs. Ramsey?"

"She was here last night. She was gone this morning. She not answering her cell phone."

"Could she have run away?"

"No. She was looking forward to going her older sister's house today and seeing her niece."

"Does she have a boyfriend?"

"Yes."

"What's his name?"

"Doug Silk."

"The quarterback?"

"Yes. Lisa is a cheerleader."

Doug Silk was one of the best quarterbacks the state had produced and was being recruited by most of the big schools. The hope was that he would play for the Minnesota Gophers.

"Did you call his house?"

"No. I'll call them and call you back."

"Good luck," the chief said.

Mrs. Silk answered the phone and told her that their son was also missing. They were hoping he had spent the night with Lisa or a friend, but it wasn't like him to not tell them where he was.

They hung up and Mrs. Ramsey called the chief back.

Chief Johanson told her it was too early to put out a bulletin for missing persons. “I’m sure they’ll turn up today,” he assured her. He was right – they would turn up.

*Francine left for work* a little before eight. Jonathan arrived with Laddie shortly after. The boys took the dogs to the trail behind his house to look for the shells. Orlando had kept the open shells from the microwave. He let the two pups smell the two shells and then let them loose. The pups went to work.

A couple of minutes later Laddie returned with a stick. They walked the trail for a good half hour without any luck. Just when they were ready to turn around, Storm barked and then came running. He dropped one of the shells at Orlando’s feet. The shell began twitching on the ground.

Orlando picked it up and said, “We need to hurry.” The boys and dogs ran back to the house with the shell in Orlando’s hand. He could feel the shell trying to open.

They made it to the house and Orlando hurried into the kitchen and placed the urp into the microwave.

“Do you have your phone?” he asked Jonathan.

“Yeah. Don’t you have yours?”

“We both should record it in case one is bad.”

“Good idea.”

“I’m going to open the door and film until it opens and we see the creature, then we’ll close the door and turn it on,” Orlando explained.

Orlando went to the silverware drawer and got out a butter knife and began trying to pry the shell open. Once he got it partially open, he quit and waited. It wasn’t long before the creature pushed it open, and it stuck its eye out and looked around. Orlando had placed it near the back of the oven hoping it would crawl out so they could get a good recording of it.

It did just as he hoped. The creature crawled out and looked up at them. It smiled. Its eye extended toward them and its two arms came out of its body. Both boys were recording. It then started toward them. Orlando slammed the microwave door shut. He started to push the button to nuke him, but Jonathan grabbed his hand and said, "Wait. What if we keep it in there and show the government man the real thing? It can't get out of there can it?"

"I wouldn't think so," Orlando answered. "That's not a bad idea."

"Let's call John and ask him," Jonathan said.

The creature had its eye up against the glass door looking for a way to get out and eat the boys' livers.

Orlando called John's cell phone.

"This is John Dunbar."

"This is Orlando and Jonathan." Orlando went on and told Mr. Dunbar that they had a monster trapped in the microwave.

"We took videos of the monster and were going to nuke it, but then Jonathan said maybe we should save it to show the government man," Orlando explained.

"I'll be right there," John Dunbar said.

*Mrs. Stella Ross* ran the operation of the community pool. The pool opened at ten. She was always there by nine. She opened the concession area and looked out and saw clothes lying by the side of the pool. She knew she had cleaned the area before she had left the day before.

She was angry that people had snuck into the pool and then left their clothes behind. She walked out and picked up the clothing, noticing that their underwear was also there. Gross, she thought. She then noticed the two shapes in the water. She screamed!

***John Dunbar arrived*** at the Gomez house and Orlando let him in. He led John into the kitchen. John looked into the microwave. The creature turned toward him and smiled. John took a step back.

"You think he could get out if we left him in there until the guy arrives?"

"I don't think so. Maybe we should take the microwave to my house."

"Okay." They unplugged it and John carried it to his car. It wasn't a very big microwave. The monster moved all around the inside its confinement looking for a way out.

His phone rang as he placed the appliance in his back seat. He closed the back door and dug the phone out of his pocket.

"There are two dead bodies in the pool!" Mrs. Ross yelled.

After trying to calm Stella, he hung up and called 911.

He then told the boys, "Stella Ross just found two bodies in the pool." The boys hopped into his car, and they drove quickly to John's house. He unloaded the microwave and placed it in his kitchen.

"You boys stay here and watch that thing. I have to go to the pool," John directed.

"Did Mrs. Ross say who it was in the pool?" Orlando asked.

"She didn't say." He left.

"You think the monsters got them?" Jonathan asked Orlando.

"I would think so since there are two bodies."

"But everyone was warned not to go out after dark," Jonathan said.

"Algunas personas son idiotas," Orlando said.

"What does that mean?"

"Some people are idiots," Orlando told him.

Mrs. Dunbar walked into the kitchen and looked into the strange microwave and screamed.

*John Dunbar arrived* at the pool at the same time as the cops showed up. Chief Johanson pulled up beside John.

The chief asked, "What do we have?"

"I just got here. All I was told is that there are two bodies in the pool."

Chief Johanson thought of the call he had gotten about the two missing teenagers. They followed the other policemen into the pool area. They all looked down at the bodies in the pool.

Mrs. Ross was sitting on a chair crying.

"Chief, this must be their clothes," one of the deputies called out. He went over as the deputy went through the pants looking for a billfold. The deputy pulled it out and handed it to the chief.

Chief Johanson opened the billfold and saw the name Douglas S. Silk on the driver's license.

"It's Doug Silk, the quarterback, and Lisa Ramsey," he said.

"How do you know her name?" John asked.

"The two of them were reported missing this morning. I can't believe I have to tell two sets of parents that their kids are dead. They had such a future."

"It looks like they were killed by the monsters," the deputy said.

"How did they the kids get in here?" the chief asked, clearly upset.

"They must have hopped the fence during the night. We have no trespassing signs all around the fence," John said, defensively.

The chief called for the forensics team before removing the bodies from the pool. The pool was closed for the day. Mrs. Ross was told to go home. An hour later as they were pulling the bodies out of the pool, a man showed his credentials and entered the pool area.

He walked up to Chief Johanson and said, "My name is Ted Wilson. I'm with the Department of Defense," while flashing his credentials.

"What? Why are you here?"

"We got word that there are strange creatures terrorizing the neighborhood. I'm here from Washington checking it out." He walked over to the two bodies and removed the sheet that covered them. He saw how both bodies had their stomachs ripped open.

"Is this the same thing that happened to the other victims?" he asked.

"Yes," Chief Johanson said. "Their livers had been removed. We suspect we'll find that the same thing is true here."

"I never liked liver," Ted said.

"Is that supposed to be funny?" Chief Johanson asked.

"Just a fact, chief," Ted Wilson said. "Give me the facts."

Chief Johanson spent the next twenty minutes telling him about the other murders and about the animals.

"All of them only had their livers removed?"

"That's correct."

"Do we have any video of these monsters?"

"No."

"Why didn't you place infrared cameras around the community to capture them on film?"

"We don't have that capability. We're a small-town police force."

"I have one of the monsters captured in my house, Mr. Wilson," John said.

Chief Johanson shot John Dunbar a look that could have killed. John ignored it.

"I'll be taking over this investigation, Chief. Also, do not tell the parents how their children died. If it got out in the papers it would cause a full-scale panic."

Chief Johanson looked like someone had stepped on his little toe.

"Fine. Good luck. If you need our assistance, call me." He knew he would have to make up something, maybe tell the parents that the kids had drowned.

"Thank you. Let's go see your monster, Mr. Dunbar."

Ted Wilson followed John to his house. As they walked inside, Orlando and Jonathan greeted them. John introduced the boys and told Ted that they had captured the monster.

"You guys?"

"Yes, sir," Orlando said.

"Is it safe for me to see this monster?"

"Yes. It's inside the microwave," Jonathan said.

"What?"

"We'll show you," Orlando told him. They walked him into the kitchen.

The monster had grown to six inches long and was pushing on the door when Ted Wilson looked through the glass.

The monster smiled at Ted and then popped his arms out of his body and tried to reach for him. Ted took a step back. He took his camera from his pocket and began taking pictures. The creature moved away from the glass and then extended his eye toward Ted to get a better look.

"How big does this thing get?"

"We've seen it around seven feet long and around three feet diameter. They seem to be able to shrink and then quickly go back to their original size. See that shell in the back of the oven?"

Ted looked closer and said, "Yes."

"He came out of that. We found it this morning in the woods," Orlando said.

Jonathan added, "John and Sam McGill have led search parties to find and destroy those. They've found dozens. We think the monsters deposit them."

"Let's go to the table and have a discussion," Ted said.

"What do you want us to do with this one?" Orlando asked. "We nuked the last two we found."

Ted laughed and said, "You nuked them. What happened?"

Jonathan said, "They exploded."

Once they were seated, Ted asked John, "How did you guys get rid of the shells."

John told him about taking them to the funeral home and having them cremated.

"I really should call Sam and have him come over. He's been my partner in this, and he was the first person to encounter the creature," John said.

Sam got the call and made a quick trip to John's house.

He saw the monster in the microwave on his way to the table. For the next two hours, the men and boys told Ted the entire story, step-by-step, of what had happened in the past few days.

When they were done, Ted said, "You guys have done a remarkable job with this. Too bad the local police haven't been more help. We're going to take over everything now. Without your diligence I'm sure many more people would have been killed."

"Thank you," Sam and John both said. Sam added, "I wish they all would have taken our advice."

"I need to make calls and get a team here." He then handed out cards to each of the four. "Call me with info or questions."

"What about the creature in the microwave?" Orlando asked.

"Let's leave it there until I can get our scientists here to study it."

# Chapter 17

*Sam offered the boys* a ride home, but they told him they wanted to walk after sitting so long at the table.

"This is kind of like in the movie *ET*," Orlando said to Jonathan.

"Hey, it is. I wonder if they will set up a big white tent," Jonathan said.

"Maybe. It's too bad about that couple that were killed," Orlando said.

"I wonder who they were," Jonathan said. Ted and John hadn't informed the boys of the identity of the bodies, only that the two had been killed the same way as Rufus and Sean.

"I wonder if Rhonda Lewis saw anything. She lives right beside the pool," Jonathan said.

"Let's go talk to her." They turned onto Ash Street and walked to her house. They rang the bell.

A few moments later Rhonda answered the door.

"Hi, Orlando, Jonathan," she greeted.

"Come in." She then asked, "What's going on at the pool?"

"Are you supposed to work today?"

"No. My day off." Rhonda wore short pajamas. Her legs distracted the boys. They took seats in the living room.

"They found two bodies in the pool this morning," Orlando told her.

"Oh, no!"

"Did you see or hear anything last night?" Jonathan asked.

"I always check the pool before going to bed. Usually around eleven. I went out on the patio to look and there were four monsters in the yard. I barely made it back into the house. It scared me so bad that I had trouble sleeping all night. I finally got to sleep early this morning. That's why I'm still in my pj's. Who were they?"

"They wouldn't tell us."

"Every so often kids from school will sneak into the pool during the night to skinny dip. I've run off them a few times, but I'm sure I don't catch all of them. I don't watch the pool all night."

"A group from the Department of Defense has taken over the investigation. We should call him. He'll want to talk to you."

"Okay," Rhonda said.

Orlando pulled out his cell phone and dialed the number on the card.

Ted answered, "This is Ted Wilson."

"Mr. Wilson, this is Orlando. We have someone you need to talk to."

Orlando gave him her address and he said he would be right there.

"I had better get dressed before he gets here."

"Okay. He's a good guy," Orlando told her. She walked them to the door. When she opened it, Spencer was riding his bike up the street. He saw them and yelled out, "Hey! You guys trying to steal my girlfriend?!"

Rhonda yelled back, "I am not your girlfriend, and stop saying that." She closed the door.

Spencer rode up to his buddies and said, "I've been looking everywhere for you guys. I didn't think you guys would be hitting on my girl."

"Did you not just hear what she said?" Jonathan told him.

"She's a little shy about it."

"And you're in la-la land," Orlando said.

"So, what else have you guys been doing, and what is happening at the pool?"

On the walk back to Orlando's house they told him everything that had happened.

"You trapped a monster in the microwave? Cool!"

*By that evening* word had spread throughout the community that the Department of Defense was here to rid the neighborhood of the monsters. They set up infrared cameras in backyards and down trails in the woods.

The boys watched as a team put up a large white tent in the park. They took over the meeting house. They had a man posted at the entrance to The Woods, not letting anyone in that didn't live in the neighborhood.

Francine got home a little after four-thirty. She saw the boys near the pool. She stopped to talk to them.

"We're just watching," Orlando said.

Ted happened to walk out of the tent at that time and saw Orlando talking to someone he figured was his mother. He walked over to the car.

"You must be Mrs. Gomez. I'm Ted Wilson. Orlando told me about the encounter you guys had with the creature. Could I come by this evening to interview you about the encounter?"

"Of course. How about you join us for dinner? We could talk while we eat."

"That would be nice if it's not too much trouble."

"No trouble at all. Say seven-thirty."

"See you then. Thanks." He walked away.

"You got a date, Mrs. Gomez," Spencer said.

Francine just shook her head and left.

"You big doofus," Orlando said. "He's coming to talk about the monsters."

"That was his excuse," Spencer said. "He could see that your mom is hot."

"You know you're sick, don't you?" Orlando told him.

Orlando's mom was hot. She was dark skinned with dark hair down to her shoulders. She was thin and fit. She had beautiful eyes and a nice smile.

August rode up on her bike. "Hi, August," Orlando said. "What have you been doing today?"

"Hung out with April. We watched the tent go up from my room. It's awful about the two people who drown in the pool."

"How did you know about that?"

"It's all over the news. The news is calling it suspicious. Both were excellent swimmers according to their parents."

"They were killed by the monsters," Spencer spurted out.

"What?!"

"We're supposed to keep that to ourselves, knucklehead," Jonathan said.

"You told me," Spencer said.

Orlando told August, "They don't want that info getting out to the public. They think it will cause a panic."

"Okay," she said.

***The Microwave with the monster inside*** was taken from John's house to the meeting house where the scientists and specialists were studying it. They all agreed that they had never come across anything like it before. They had no clue where it could have come from. They erected a ten-by-ten glass cube in the meeting house after removing the chairs.

They placed the microwave inside the door and opened it. The monster came out and quickly grew to six feet. The observers moved away from the glass. The creature began scaling the walls with its suctioned feet trying to find a way out. It walked upside down on the ceiling, all the while leaving a slime as it went. They placed a chicken inside the glass cage and watched as the creature enveloped it and ripped its stomach open to remove the liver. It engulfed the liver and then shrunk back to earthworm size and crawled under the microwave.

The watchers stood in amazement. They filmed the entire thing and sent it to Washington to be analyzed.

Ted Wilson met with each of the leaders of their groups at six inside the tent. They went over plans for the night. They had eight men who would canvass the neighborhood with guns and flamethrowers. They planned to search the entire area the next morning for the urps.

"Depending on what we get tonight we may want to bait a backyard tomorrow evening with a couple of sheep. Then we will wait for them to appear," he told the group.

"Dave, contact a local farmer in the morning to see if we can purchase some sheep or goats. Guys, we are encountering something none of us have ever seen. We have no knowledge of what they are capable of. We need to be careful. I was told that the locals have sent out search parties and found dozens of the shells."

"How is any of this possible?" One of the men asked. "How can they go from worm size to seven feet and then deposit urps? Scientifically and logically it's not possible."

"The only explanation I can come up with is that it's extra-terrestrial. Does anyone else have any other ideas?"

The men sat there looking at each other.

**Francine** had just stepped out of the shower when her phone rang. She saw on the screen that it was Lucas West. She smiled and answered.

"Hello."

"Francine, this is Lucas West. We met yesterday."

"Of course. The grass mower."

Lucas laughed, "I was calling to ask you to dinner. I know it's spur of the moment."

"I'd love to, but I'm cooking dinner here. Why don't you join us? Then you can take me out another day."

"A home cooked meal sounds good. Thank you."

"Seven-thirty."

"I'll see you then."

She was surprised to hear from Lucas so soon. She had felt a connection with him and had hoped that perhaps he would ask her out. But she knew nothing about him. He could already have a special someone.

She didn't have a lot of time to plan a big dinner. She figured everyone liked Italian. She decided to make baked spaghetti with Cole slaw and French bread. She headed for the kitchen; her hair still wrapped in a towel.

*The boys* had gone to Jonathan's house to let Laddie out. Orlando then told them he needed to go home to let Storm out. When he got home, Storm met him at the door wagging his tail and jumping up on him. He walked into the kitchen and found his mom preparing dinner. He took the pup out to the backyard. He played with the dog after it had done its business.

When Orlando came back inside, Francine asked him, "Would you set the table for four?"

"Four?"

"Lucas is joining us."

"Oh yeah. You invited him?"

"No. He called and said he was coming to dinner," she laughed.

"You like him?"

"Mind your own business."

"This is kind of my business."

"No, it's not."

"Okay. Two dates at the same time."

"Set the table, and then go get ready." Before leaving, he asked Alexa to play Beatles songs. It always put his mother in a good mood.

The doorbell rang at seven-twenty. Orlando ran to the door and opened it for Ted Wilson.

"Hope I'm not too early," he said.

"Not at all, come in," Francine said as she entered the room. Storm decided to greet Ted also.

"What a great looking shepherd," Ted said as he bent down to pet the pup.

"I just got him Monday. He's great at finding the shells," Orlando told him.

"He may have to come work for the government."

"Have a seat. Dinner will be ready soon."

The doorbell rang again. Orlando opened it to see Lucas standing there with flowers. Orlando smiled and said, "Come in."

Francine walked back in and saw the confused look on Lucas's face. "Let me introduce the two of you."

"Of course," Lucas said.

"This is Lucas West. He lives on Ash Street, close to the pool. Lucas, this is Ted Wilson with the Department of Defense."

Lucas was cool. He shook hands. Never questioned why another man was invited to dinner. "I'm just finishing up. It will be ready soon."

Lucas handed her the mixed bouquet of flowers.

"Thank you. They are beautiful."

Francine had put on a flowered sundress. She left her hair hanging on her shoulders. She looked very nice. She even wore a light trace of makeup, even though she didn't need it.

The men talked about the pup as it went from one person to the other to get petted.

"How is everything going?" Lucas asked.

"It may be the strangest case I've been on. It has everyone stumped. But we'll figure it out.

"Hopefully soon. It's awful what's been happening. This was a nice quiet community and now this."

"I can't imagine," Ted said.

"Dinner is ready. If you need the restroom, it's down the hall on the left," Francine told the men.

"I'm going to wash up," Ted said.

Francine told Orlando, "Put Storm in your room during dinner."

He took the pup upstairs. He then told Lucas, "You can use the upstairs bathroom."

Lucas followed him. He could quickly tell that it was Orlando's bathroom. Towels were thrown on the floor, toothpaste in the sink. It reminded him of his bathroom as a kid. He washed up and headed back to the dining room.

"I hope everyone likes baked Spaghetti. Not much time for something fancier," Francine said.

"It looks great," Lucas said.

"Can't wait to dig in," Ted told her.

Francine poured glasses of wine for herself and the men. Orlando got out a Coke.

Once they were seated and the meal began, Francine asked, "Should we begin or wait till after we eat?" Lucas looked up at them.

"Why don't we wait. It won't take long. Let's enjoy the food and the company," Ted said.

Francine explained, "Ted is here to question me about our encounter with the creature."

"I'd like to hear that," Lucas said.

"Okay. After we eat."

Orlando led the conversation during dinner talking about how he and Storm had encountered a moose. He retold the story of when they were chased down the street four days earlier. He thought it seemed like weeks since it had happened.

"Have you had any encounters, Lucas?"

"No, other than helping in the search for the shells. That was when I met Orlando and Francine."

"Well worth the time then," Ted said.

"Are there really aliens out there?" Orlando asked.

They all turned their attention to Ted.

"That is classified," Ted said.

"I'll take that as a yes," Orlando said.

"I've encountered a UFO," Lucas then said. "Whether it was alien or not, I don't know."

"Tell us," Francine said.

"I was with a group of guys up in the boundary waters on a fishing trip. We were camped on a small island sitting around the campfire one evening after dark. Suddenly, a light shone down on us out of nowhere. It lit up the entire island. Now, the island wasn't that big. Maybe sixty yards wide. We looked up and stood so we could be beamed up and taken away."

"What happened?!" Orlando nearly shouted.

"The light disappeared just as suddenly as it appeared, and we saw a disc-like object move across the horizon in front of a rising moon," Lucas finished.

"We've had folks mistake the northern lights for UFO's," Ted said.

"I've seen northern lights before. This was not that."

"I've always wanted to go to the boundary waters and the Quetico National Park," Orlando told him.

"It is beautiful," Lucas said. "And the fishing is great."

"This meal is delicious," Ted said.

"Yes, it is," Lucas added.

"Thank you both," Francine said. "It was pretty simple."

"What is the strangest thing you've seen?" Orlando asked Ted.

"Orlando, let Ted eat," Francine said.

"Sorry."

"It's okay. The strangest thing I've ever seen happened today. It's that thing. I don't even know what to call it. It defies explanation." He went on to tell why.

"So, you think it's not of this world?" Lucas asked.

"I can't say that," Ted said, and then winked.

Orlando sat up straighter in his chair. Thinking of the ramifications of that.

When they had finished the meal, Orlando cleared the table, poured each of the adults another glass of wine and put the dishes in the dishwasher while Francine talked about the creature coming into their house.

"Wow. That had to be frightening," Lucas said.

"It was."

When her story was over, Ted thanked her for a wonderful meal and said he needed to be going. "I'll have one of my men return your microwave as soon as we can."

"My microwave? Where's my microwave?" She hadn't noticed it missing.

"We caught one of the monsters in it this morning. They took it for observation."

"What?"

"It was the only way we knew to catch one and show it to Ted," Orlando explained.

"At least we didn't nuke this one to bits," Orlando said.

"What?"

“We nuked other ones earlier in the week.”

“Keep the microwave,” Francine said.

“I guess I’d better be going,” Ted said as he laughed. We’ll get you a new one.”

“Should I leave?” Lucas asked.

“Stay and have another glass of wine with me and talk. It’s nice having another adult to talk to,” Francine said.

“Thanks. I take offence at that,” Orlando said, teasing. He was happy his mom was enjoying Lucas’s company.

It was dark outside. Orlando knew he should have taken Storm out beforehand. He turned on the front light and took Storm out on the leash, keeping watch for the monster. Storm peed and then headed back to the house, like he sensed danger. Orlando was glad to head inside himself.

He and Storm went upstairs while Francine and Lucas took seats on the couch and talked. She found out he worked from home. He designed video games and did computer repairs. He had been married for ten years, and then divorced four years ago. He was a year older than Francine.

# Chapter 18

***The four monsters*** began their nightly hunt around the neighborhood. The night before had been a good night. They went back to the pool looking for more swimmers. They saw the large white tent. They sensed danger and went back into the woods as they circled the community looking for victims in the backyards.

They saw two humans in gray outfits with lights on their heads. They were carrying weapons. They were in Sam McGill's backyard. One of the monsters rushed toward the two humans out of his desire for their livers. The monster was burnt to a crisp by the flamethrowers. The three other monsters headed back into the woods to look for food.

Sam saw the light from the flames in his backyard and opened his door. He saw the two agents standing over a burnt spot in his grass. He turned on the backdoor light and stepped out. They explained what had happened as they directed their headlamps toward the spot. The three of them looked down at what was left of the creature. It wasn't much. Patsy stood at the door with her hands over her mouth.

***Meanwhile***, back near the pool in the woods, a shell cracked open. The creature began its instinctive hunt for food. It grew as it moved. By the time it reached the meeting house it was five feet long. There was a light inside the building, but it didn't hear any sound except for a hum that came from the locked-up monster in the cage.

It shrunk back to earthworm size and slithered under the door through a small crack where part of the sill had been broken and never repaired. It entered the room and increased in size and walked to the cage. It walked up the side of the cage and came face-to-face with the other monster inside. They followed each other around the cage and to the top where the caged creature was upside down. If the creature hadn't known better, it would have thought it was crawling around on a mirror.

Two guards had been hired to stand watch of the tent and the meeting house at night. The guard at the meeting house came out of the restroom after taking a long bathroom break. He saw the monster hanging from the ceiling but didn't notice the other one over him on top of the glass box. He took a seat in a chair in the middle of the room with his back to it. The thing creeped him out.

He never saw the creature until it was too late. The creature inside the box went crazy as the other monster ate the liver in front of it. The creature then shrunk back down and left, fulfilled.

Saturday

*The following morning,* they found the guard lying on the floor. They all wondered how the monster got out of the glass cage, killed the guard, and got back into the box.

Ted Wilson felt awful that the man had lost his life. During the morning meeting they had a moment of silence for him.

Also, during the meeting, the men that had searched the community with flamethrowers gave their report. They were happy to report that they had killed one of the monsters.

The cards were collected from the infrared cameras and looked at. They saw the monsters on the trail and in some of the backyards. They had film of the monster as it burned.

"It just combusted," Ted said.

"There was almost nothing left," the agent said.

Ted directed, "This morning we do a search of the entire community and woods looking for these shells." He showed everyone what the shells looked like.

"The scientists are going to continue to study the monster we have in the cage. I have a feeling it was another monster that killed the guard. I want cameras placed in the tent and the meeting house. That was my mistake not to have them already installed," Ted said.

"Why would we have thought we would need them?" one of the men said, comforting their boss.

Dave reported that they had gotten two sheep and would pick them up shortly before nightfall. They had placed a tie-off rod in the ground behind Rufus Langley's house since no one lived there any longer. They would tie a sheep to the rod after dark. The flamethrower patrol would keep guard during the night.

*Francine had a rare day off,* she slept late due to the wine she and Lucas had consumed during the evening. She hoped to see him again. She liked him.

Orlando had gotten up early to let Storm out and decided to ride his bike up to the tent. He left a note on the fridge telling his mother where he had gone. He saw some men carrying a body out of the meeting house to an ambulance. He wondered what had happened. He went on to the pool. He parked his bike at the pool bike rack and stood against the rod iron fence watching the tent for activity.

Ted Wilson came out of the tent with a couple of other agents. He looked up and saw Orlando. He said something to the men and then came over to where Orlando stood.

They greeted one another and then Orlando asked. "What happened at the meeting house? I saw them carrying a body out. I'm hoping it was the monster."

"No. The guard was attacked by a monster last night. He was found this morning the same as the others."

"Was the creature still in the box?" Orlando asked.

"Yes."

"Maybe the guard got careless and opened the door."

"The door was closed and locked this morning. So unless the monster knows how to close a door and lock it..." he didn't finish the sentence.

"What's happening today?"

"We 're going to do a thorough search of the entire area looking for the shells."

"Do you need help?"

"Sure. The more eyes the better."

"I can get my friends and I'll take Storm."

"We're starting at ten from here."

Orlando looked at his phone and saw that it was a little after nine.

"I'll be here," he told Ted.

"Please send my thanks to your mom again for dinner last night."

"Okay."

Orlando wasted no time. He got on his phone and called Jonathan. He told him to tell Spencer. He then called August and had her see if April wanted to help. He then rode his bike to Sam's house. He rang the doorbell and Patsy came to the door.

"Is Sam here?"

"Come in, Orlando. I'll go get him."

Sam entered the room and Orlando quickly told him about the search.

"I'll be there. I'll call John."

"I'm going home to get Storm. See you there."

Orlando then rode home and entered the house. His mother was in the kitchen, standing at the counter, drinking coffee.

"A guard was attacked and killed last night at the meeting house," he blurted out.

"Oh, no. By the monster?"

"Yes."

"They're doing a search this morning starting at ten. We're going to help. Do you want to help?"

"I don't know. I'm awfully tired."

"I thought maybe you could invite Lucas to help," Orlando said.

"Well maybe, I'll give him a call and see if he's busy."

"I'm going to take Storm. He's good at finding the shells. He went to get the empty shells he had, put a few cans of bear spray in his backpack and took off. He yelled out, "See you at the tent!"

Francine was on the phone with Lucas. He told her he could join her in the search. She hurried to fix her hair and get dressed. She put on cute shorts and a sleeveless top.

As Orlando was riding his bike up Maple Street, he saw Rhonda Lewis standing in front of her house. She motioned Orlando over.

"What is going on this morning?" she asked.

"The agents are conducting another search in the neighborhood. We're going to help. You want to help?"

"Okay. I'm out of a job until they reopen the pool and there's nothing else to do." Orlando walked his bike next to her.

She bent down to pet Storm. Orlando asked her, "You knew the couple that were killed in the pool, didn't you?"

"Yes. They were good friends. I was on the cheerleading team with her. It's awful. I knew they snuck into the pool occasionally, and I told them they shouldn't. They wouldn't listen."

"It's not your fault."

"It's still sad."

"I know. One of the guards was killed last night."

"They need to get rid of these monsters," Rhonda said with tears in her eyes. Orlando totally agreed with that.

They arrived at the tent a few minutes early. Jonathan and Spencer were there.

"You brought my girlfriend," Spencer said.

"You call me your girlfriend one more time, I'll have you banned from the pool," Rhonda said.

"Touchy," Spencer said.

Ted Wilson assigned different groups to different streets, much like John and Sam had done. "If you have any questions about whether the shells you find are what we're looking for, just keep them. It's better to be wrong than leave one behind. Good luck."

Hardly any of the creature's urps had been found on Maple Street, except for the cul-de-sac. Almost all of them had been found in backyards near the forest.

Orlando showed his shells to August, April, and Rhonda.

"This is what they look like," he said.

August and Rhonda searched with Orlando, and April went with Jonathan and Spencer. They all were in the same group but while Orlando's group was searching backyards, the others were assigned to front and side yards.

They headed around Ash Street.

Other groups of people were going down Maple Street and then right onto Oak Street. Francine and Lucas were in that group. Orlando had given his mom one of the empty shells. Francine was happy to see Lucas so soon after their pleasant evening.

"I had a good time last night," Lucas told her as they searched.

"So did I," she said with a grin.

"Perhaps I could take you on a proper date?" he asked. "Dinner and a movie?"

"I would like that," she said. "Is this one?" she asked as she bent down and picked up an urp.

"It looks like one to me," Lucas said. She handed it to Lucas, and he put it in his pocket.

"Did you bring bear spray?" she asked.

"No. Why?"

"Almost everyone carries bear spray in the neighborhood because of the bears in the area."

"Didn't know that." She pulled out one of the two bottles she had and gave it to him.

"You are now prepared to protect me from a bear," she said.

"I didn't realize I moved into such a dangerous neighborhood."

"Keep your eye on the single women."

"I am," he said, flirtingly.

She blushed.

Storm came up to Orlando and dropped a shell at his feet.

"Good boy," he said and patted his head. He gave Storm a treat. Storm took off for the edge of the woods again.

"It's hard to imagine that the monsters I saw came out of that thing," Rhonda said.

"I know. It's wild," August said.

The search lasted three hours. Orlando's group found twenty-three shells. A dozen of them were found by Storm. The other group found ten.

Ted Wilson had led a group around the main trail in the woods and found a grand total of five. That was thirty-eight shells that would never be hatched into monsters.

Ted told the volunteers, "Thank you so much for helping. Tonight, we hope to rid your community of all the existing monsters."

Everyone applauded.

"Do you really believe we found all the shells?" Rhonda asked Orlando.

"No. Why would we find twenty-three while the other group only found ten?"

"You're right. That doesn't make sense."

"I think I'll take Storm for a walk around the backyards they searched," Orlando said.

"I've got to get home," Rhonda said.

"Me too," August said as she kissed Orlando's cheek. "I'll walk with you," she told Rhonda.

As the two girls walked together, Rhonda said, "You really like Orlando, don't you?"

"Yeah. He's great," she said.

"He is," Rhonda agreed.

Jonathan and Spencer asked Orlando what he was going to do. He told them his plan and Jonathan said he would go with him. Spencer said he was tired and headed home.

Before Lucas left Francine for home he said, "How about this evening?"

"What?"

"Our date. Could you go this evening?"

"I guess I could."

"I'll pick you up at six. Dress casual."

"See you then," she said.

Orlando, Jonathan and Storm began their own search. They searched all the backyards on Oak Street and found fourteen more shells, ten were found by Storm. He loved all the puppy treats.

After the search, the boys took the shells up to the tent, after dropping off Storm, and asked for Ted Wilson. Ted came out and the boys handed him the fourteen shells. "We found these in the backyards the other group had searched. They didn't have Storm," giving the group an excuse.

"Thank you. You boys want to come in," Ted asked.

The boys were excited to see inside the tent. There were tables set up with men running around from table to table. It looked like they were doing experiments on the shells. Theboys couldn't understand much of what was going on there. There were parts of the tent that were partitioned off.

"We're examining different materials found around the monsters and parts of the monsters. The slime has been examined."

"What have you determined?"

"Can't tell you that," Ted said.

Jonathan said, "It's aliens, isn't it?"

Ted ignored the question.

"It's the only thing that makes sense," Jonathan continued.

Ted took them from the tent to the meeting house where the monster was still locked in the glass container. It was nowhere to be seen.

"Where is it?" Orlando asked.

"During the day it shrinks and hides under the microwave," Ted said.

Their microwave still sat in the middle of the cube.

"It is the most unusual thing I've ever come across. It has the people in Washington scratching their heads."

"Have there been any reports of these creatures in other parts of the country, or the world?" Orlando asked.

"No. Thank God," Ted said.

"Then why here?" Jonathan asked.

"Just unlucky I guess," he answered.

After touring the tent and meeting house, the boys took off for home. They both were worn out.

Orlando said his goodbye as Jonathan turned toward his house. Orlando continued home. Storm was still asleep in the living room on his bed.

Orlando went into the kitchen to find something to eat. He made a peanut butter and jelly sandwich and went to turn on the Twins game. They were playing an afternoon game against the Yankees.

Francine came down and sat with him on the couch.

"Lucas invited me to dinner and a movie." He looked at her and smiled.

"What's that smile about?"

"I knew you liked him."

"He's very nice," she said.

"Should I expect you back tonight or in the morning?" he asked.

"What kind of woman do you think I am?"

"One who hasn't had a partner in years," Orlando said.

She knew he was right. An overnight stay sounded like fun, but she said, "This is our first date. I'll be home early. Dinner and a movie is all. He's picking me up at six."

"Okay."

Orlando fell asleep on the couch during the seventh inning.

He woke up when the doorbell rang. He got up to answer the door. Lucas West stood there. Orlando invited him in.

Orlando yelled down the hall, "Mom, your date is here."

"It's going to be an interesting night," Lucas said.

Orlando didn't know how to take the statement. Was he talking about the evening with his mother or something else?

Lucas saw the confused look on Orlando's face and said, "I mean with the agents placing the sheep out and trying to eliminate the monsters."

"I'd like to see that."

“See what?” Francine asked as she entered the room. She looked fantastic. Orlando couldn’t even believe it was his mother. She had on tight jeans with a light sweater. Her hair looked the best he had ever seen it. It seemed to him that she was the one setting the trap tonight.

“I was talking about the agents hunting the monsters tonight with the sheep.”

“Don’t you dare go out to see that.”

“I know better than that, Mom.”

“Oh, I’m sorry, Orlando. I didn’t fix you any dinner.”

“It’s okay, Mom. I think there’s some stale bread and water in the kitchen.”

“Then he’ll be fine,” Lucas jumped in.

“Very funny,” she said.

“I’ll be okay, Mom. Have fun. Don’t worry about your only child going without food tonight.”

“Bye,” she said.

Once they were in Lucas’s car, he said, “What a great kid.”

“He really is. Smart aleck, but he is a great son,” she said. “He’s had to take on a lot of responsibilities.”

# Chapter 19

*Once it was dark,* the agents went out searching the community for the monsters armed with guns and flamethrowers. Folks watched from their windows as the men walked down the streets looking as if they were invading the neighborhood.

Two of the agents led a sheep to the backyard of Rufus Langley. They tied it off to the rod they had planted and then hid inside the house with the back door open. They would rush out once they saw the monsters get close to the animal.

The agents did not know how many monsters were left. They thought there were three, but there could be more. No one knew if other shells had hatched. Their hope was that they had found most, if not all, the shells during the search that morning.

*Three of the creatures* had awoken and began their raid on the community. They didn't realize that three other shells had been sprung open earlier that evening and were now also roaming the area. The three new creatures had not yet met up with the other three. They searched for food alone. One of them had found a squirrel soon after escaping the shell and had its first taste of liver. It wanted more.

Two agents were searching Elm Street around ten-thirty when they came face-to-face with one of the newly hatched creatures. The creature ran toward them. They both fired their flamethrowers and the creature collapsed in a heap and ignited. Its eye leaped from its head as though watching itself burn. The men were traumatized from the sight.

***Around eleven,*** Francine arrived back home after her date with Lucas West. She had a fantastic time. She found Lucas very easy to talk to, a perfect gentleman, and more handsome than she had at first thought. She was very much attracted to him.

He pulled into her driveway and got out of the car to walk her to her door. Orlando was watching through a slat of their door shades. He didn't like the fact that he had gotten out of the car. Didn't he know there were monsters around?

Lucas walked her to the door and said, "I had a terrific time."

"Me too," she said. He leaned in to kiss her. As their lips met Orlando opened the door.

"Don't you two realize there are monsters out there? Come inside if you want to do that."

"I'll see you soon," Francine said.

"He's right. I'd better get home," Lucas said.

It had been one week ago that the first creature appeared to Sam McGill and chased the boys up the street. So much had gone on since then. The killings and dead animals. Orlando felt as though it had been a month or longer.

He now had a pup named Storm. He had a girlfriend named August, and his mother was dating a guy named Lucas.

Sunday

***It was after midnight*** when the three creatures finally appeared in Rufus's backyard. The two agents waited until the creatures were five feet from the sheep. It was baaing like crazy with fright, as the monsters approached with caution. The agents rushed out the door toward the sheep. The monsters seemed confused at first. They wanted the liver the sheep had to offer; they wanted the liver the two humans had. Their instincts told them they should flee, but they didn't.

The three creatures quickly separated. One went toward the sheep, the other two toward the men. The agents fired their flamethrowers. The two creatures who had made the wrong decision to rush the men, now lay in a heap of ash. The third monster rushed into the woods with the men chasing them. The agents knew better than to use the flamethrowers in the woods. They didn't want a major forest fire on their hands. There hadn't been rain in the area for the past ten days. The forest was dry. They took out their guns and began firing at the thing. It shrunk quickly in size behind a large boulder and then hid under a small rock. The men couldn't find it, even with their flashlights.

Two other agents saw another monster behind Ruth Johnson's house. They terminated it. The agents spent the rest of the night walking the community, hoping to find other monsters. When the light of day appeared, they quit and headed for the meeting house.

**Orlando spent a restless night** in bed. Each time he would fall asleep he would soon be awakened again from another nightmare. His last nightmare had Storm rushing out the front door as Francine came home from her date. A creature was waiting for him around the corner of the house. Before Orlando could get to him, Storm's liver had already been removed. The monster looked at Orlando and smiled. Orlando wanted to rip the creature apart from eye to tail. But he awoke.

Orlando got up with the sun, left a note for his mother, and took off on his bike to the meeting house. He wanted to know how many monsters had been killed. He wanted to know if the sheep had been killed. He wanted to know what the plan was now.

As he stood outside the meeting house, he took out his phone and called Ted Wilson. Ted directed the guard at the door to let Orlando inside.

Once Orlando was inside the building, he saw the agents sitting around a large table with Ted at the head of it. He looked up and saw Orlando standing there.

"Come over and pull up a chair," Ted said.

Orlando couldn't believe it was happening. He walked toward the table as one of the agents grabbed a chair and slid it next to Ted.

"Agents, this is Orlando Gomez. He's been very helpful in our mission. His dog, Storm, found nearly two dozen of the shells yesterday."

The men around the table applauded. Orlando counted twelve agents. Including Ted Wilson.

"We were just starting our report from last night's search. Who has kills?"

An agent with a crewcut and thick neck raised his hand and said, "We encountered three of the monsters at the sheep stakeout. We killed two of them with the flamethrowers and the third escaped into the woods. We gave chase until he disappeared.

"He shrunk," Orlando said to Ted.

"What?" Ted asked.

"The monster shrunk just like the one in the glass cage does," Orlando said.

"You're probably right. Next."

Another thin agent about the size of Orlando spoke, "Jake and I encountered one around ten-thirty on Elm Street. We killed it with our flamethrowers. But as it burned its eye popped forward and watched itself burn. It was the spookiest thing I had ever seen."

There was a buzz around the table.

"Anyone else?" Ted asked.

An agent at the opposite end of the table said he had seen one of the creatures, but it was too far away for the flamethrower. Before he could raise his rifle, the creature disappeared back into the woods.

"Where was this at?"

"Behind a house on the west end of Oak Street behind the cul-de-sac," the agent said.

"Anything else?"

"What's on the agenda for the day?" one of the agents asked.

"You guys can head to the hotel and get some food and sleep. Report back at six this evening. I'll have a plan then. We will need to keep hunting the monsters. We knew there were three going into last night. From your accounts you saw five and eliminated three of them, which means there are still two out there, probably more."

The men nodded.

"Orlando, you got anything?"

He looked shocked, "Uh, maybe one thing. It seems the most success came from tying the sheep up in the backyard. Instead of roaming the neighborhood, why not tie up sheep, or chickens, or pigs in several back yards and wait for the monsters to come to you guys. The monsters are searching for food. They will find the animals."

"He's right. I'll get more animals today. Meeting adjourned. Get some rest," Ted said.

The agents rose and left the building. Ted looked over at Orlando and said, "That was very astute of you. You're right."

"I worry that each night as the monsters are out, they are dropping more of the shells. How will you ever get rid of all of them?" Orlando said.

"I don't know. We need more Storms," Ted said, referring to Orlando's German Sheperd pup.

"What are you doing today?" Orlando asked.

"I have a lot going on with the research, and I'll need to contact the farmer we got the sheep from and see if we can buy more animals."

"Thanks for letting me sit at the table. That was neat."

"Thanks for the suggestion."

Orlando left the building after looking at their microwave sitting in the middle of the glass cage. He turned and asked Ted, "Have you guys fed the monster since it's been in there?"

"No."

"How long do you think they'd live without food or water?"

"At least three days," Ted said, with little concern.

They had placed the creature in the cage on Friday, it was now Sunday.

Orlando left the building and headed home. He was hoping his mother was up fixing breakfast. He was hungry.

He had been negligent about mowing yards the past week. He had four customers in the community that paid him to mow their yards. It was a way he could help his mother with the bills. He liked mowing and didn't mind giving her the money. She had provided everything he needed.

He decided to get some breakfast and head out to mow the yards. When he got home, he found his mother sitting at the table eating a muffin.

"Muffins?"

"On top of the stove."

They were blueberry muffins. He grabbed three and put them on a plate, got a glass of milk from the fridge and took a seat at the table.

"The blackberries should be ripe," Francine said.

"I need to mow yards today," Orlando said.

"Maybe I'll go pick some. I don't have to be at work until three this afternoon," she said.

"I bet Lucas would help you if you asked. Especially if you promised him a blackberry pie."

"He might," she said and grinned.

"You had a really good time last night, didn't you?"

"What makes you say that?"

"You seem happier this morning."

She ignored him and asked, "Did you learn anything this morning?"

"The agents killed three of the monsters last night."

"That's good, isn't it? Is that all of them?"

"They saw two others that got away."

"Will this ever end?" Francine asked.

"I don't know."

After eating and taking Storm out to play for a while, Orlando took the mower and trimmer out of the garage and headed to Ruth Johnson's house to mow. She paid him fifteen dollars to mow her yard. All the other customers paid him twenty, and sometimes twenty-five. Orlando knew his price was too cheap. He knew some folks in the neighborhood were paying lawn services up to fifty and sixty dollars to mow and trim their grass. But his customers were loyal, and it helped his mom.

*Francine called Lucas* and invited him to pick blackberries with her. The patch was large, and she usually got around a gallon of berries on a pick.

"Berry picking, huh? Is that a euphuism for something else?"

Francine laughed and said, "No. Just good old berry picking. There might be a pie in it for you."

"I love pie," he said.

"Good, see you soon. Wear clothing that will cover your arms and legs," she told him.

Fifteen minutes later he was there. In her excitement at seeing him again, she forgot the bear spray. They walked into the woods behind her house and down a trail for nearly a half a mile before coming to the patch. It was full of ripe blackberries ready for picking.

"Wow. Look at these," he said.

"The rule is you have to put more in the bucket than you eat," she told him.

"I didn't realized Hoyle had rules for blackberry picking."

Before they started picking, he leaned in for a kiss. It had been so long since she had felt that urge, she thought. She took a deep breath and let it out. It took all the resolution she had to not lay him down under one of the nearby trees.

She hoped this would be considered their second date. She anxiously awaited their third date.

As they picked, they talked. Francine told Lucas what Orlando was doing and that she had to work later that day. Lucas told her about his parents and younger sister and her family in Minneapolis.

It was a bit overcast and felt like it could rain that evening. They had picked the entire patch in around an hour. Their buckets were full. They came out of the brambles with scratches on their hands and arms, despite having long sleeves on.

They were admiring the berries they had picked when they heard a low growl. They turned and looked at a large black bear twenty yards behind them. He seemed very upset at them for stealing his berries.

Francine reached into her pants pocket for the bear spray. Her pockets were empty. How stupid, she told herself.

"Let's sit one of the buckets down on the ground and leave it for him and back away around the patch," Lucas said.

"Good idea."

Lucas slowly took her bucket, which had fewer berries, and placed it down on the ground. They began backing away as they moved to the backside of the patch. The bear moved forward, his nose twitching. He made his way to the bucket of berries and began eating them. Francine and Lucas made a hasty getaway.

"That was exciting," Lucas said as they walked back toward the community.

"It was scary. That was a big bear. I can't believe I forgot the spray," she said.

"Now I realize why everyone carries the spray."

"It's too bad you gave the bear the berries for your pie," she teased.

"If I remember correctly. We left *your* berries for the bear."

"Perhaps you would share them with me," she said.

***Meanwhile,*** Orlando had finished mowing Ruth's yard. He knocked on the door and waited for Mrs. Johnson to answer. She opened the door and invited him in. He saw the two cats lying in a chair in the living room.

"How are the cats?"

"They seem happy. Fluffy is a little more relaxed than Mittens. Mittens likes to get into things."

Ruth opened her purse and handed him a twenty-dollar bill.

"I'm sorry, Mrs. Johnson. But I don't have any change with me."

"With the price of gasoline these days I think you need a raise. Keep it."

"Thank you, Mrs. Johnson. Have a nice day."

Orlando left and headed to Bill and Helen Miller's house, at the other end of the street. They had left for church and come home as he was finishing up. They thanked him and gave him twenty-five dollars. He headed down Maple Street to a house across from Spencer's house.

As he was mowing the yard, Spencer walked across the street and said, "What's you doing?"

Orlando just looked at him, knowing Spencer didn't need an answer to that question.

"Want to do something after you get done?"

"Sure. I have one more yard to mow after this one," Orlando said. "I'll call you later."

It was almost one by the time he finished the yard. He headed for the last yard. He arrived home an hour before his mom had to leave for work. He dropped ninety dollars on the table. Francine picked up the money and took it to her bedroom. He didn't know she had been putting all his mowing money into a savings account for his college fund.

When she came back, he asked, "Mom, could we go out for lunch before you have to go to work."

"I guess so. Where would you like to go, McDonalds?"

"No. I don't want fast food. How about that little café in town?"

"Libby's?"

"Yeah. I like it."

"Okay. Go wash up and change. You've got grass all over you."

Ten minutes later he came down and they left for the café.

# *Chapter 20*

***Eleven urps were opening*** in the woods that afternoon. The urps had been dropped in spots away from the trails that had never been searched. The worms emerged from their shells and hid beneath leaves and in crevices until nightfall. Little did they know there wasn't enough food for all of them, and they evidently didn't have the intelligence to venture outside the small community.

***Ted Wilson had a conference call*** with his superiors in Washington.

"What can you tell us about the situation there?" his boss asked.

His boss, his boss's boss, and many other department heads were on the call, including the vice president of the United States of America.

"As of now we are controlling the situation. We destroyed three more creatures last night. We have a plan in place tonight to hopefully rid the area of the rest of them."

"Reports have been making the national news about the people killed there. They want a reason why. Is there any thought of completely burning the community and forest down to destroy the monsters?" the vice president asked.

"No, Mr. Vice President." Ted thought how could he even offer such a horrible idea.

"You now believe these monsters are from outer space?" the vice president asked.

"We have no other explanation for the creatures. We have never come across anything like this," Ted told him. He didn't want to come right out and say that was what he believed.

Ted's boss then asked, "Should we send more people up there? We really need to contain this soon. We can't have these monsters invading other areas."

"If these creatures were dropped here by aliens, then we may not be able to control the spread. They could be dropped everywhere," Ted said.

The people on the other end of the line went quiet.

Finally, Ted's boss said, "That's a lot to take in."

"Hopefully our scientists can come up with an easier way to eliminate the creature than to have to hunt them down and kill them."

The vice president then said to Ted's boss, "I believe you should head up there with more men and see this for yourself. Call in the National Guard if you need to."

"Yes, sir, Mr. Vice President."

After hanging up, Ted wanted to throw something. He didn't need a bunch of people here. Sure, he might be able to use more agents for hunting the creatures. But more bureaucrats tended to gum up the works. Bringing in others made it look like he couldn't handle his job. He didn't think anyone else could handle this situation any better.

"I'll have the turkey sandwich on country bread and a bowl of chicken noodle soup," Orlando told the waitress. Francine ordered the chef's salad.

"It's nice having this time with you. It's been so crazy this past week," Francine said. "Thanks for suggesting it."

"Thanks again for letting me get Storm."

"He's a great dog. Who knew he would be a hero?"

"Ruth Johnson wanted me to thank you again for taking her to get the cats. She is crazy over them."

"She's a sweet lady."

Their food was delivered, and they began eating.

"What are you doing the rest of the day? This is my late shift. I won't be home until almost midnight."

"I don't know. Probably fool around with Jonathan and Spencer. I was supposed to call Spencer after I got done with the mowing. Oh well."

"Just be careful. Text me if you need anything."

They finished their meals and went for ice cream at the Dairy Queen. Orlando got a chocolate cone dipped in chocolate.

Spencer was on his bike near Orlando's house when they pulled into the driveway. Once Spencer saw Orlando licking the cone he asked, "Where's mine?"

"Back at the DQ. We would have brought it, but I knew it would melt before we got it to you."

"You should have taken me."

"Come on, let's call Jonathan."

"His family went to visit his mom's aunt. He said they would be back soon."

Francine left for work. Spencer and Orlando took Storm out in the backyard to play fetch.

Once Jonathan got home, Orlando asked his two friends if they wanted to spend the night. They got permission and they played video games until dark.

**Ted Wilson had bought** six chickens, two goats, and two small pigs from the same farmer they had gotten the other two sheep.

Just before dark, each agent took an animal and tied it in a resident's backyard. They had collected each resident's cell phone number from John Dunbar, and then texted them that this was happening.

This was the big night. Ted's hope was that they would rid the community of all the monsters during the night. No way did he know about the eleven new monsters that had joined the hunt.

One of the agents came to the front door. He recognized Orlando.

"Orlando, I'm agent Hawkins, I'm placing a pig in the back yard. Can I wait inside the back door?"

"Sure. Can we help with anything?"

"I don't think so. I'll let you know. No telling how long it will be before the creature comes."

"How about something to drink while you wait?"

"Ice water would be nice."

"There's a bathroom down the hall if you need it," Orlando told him.

The agent took the pig to the back and tied him up to a metal rod he screwed into the dirt. He then went inside to wait.

Spencer went in and took a seat at the kitchen table and asked the agent, "How long have you been an agent?"

"Six years."

"How old are you?"

"Twenty-eight."

"How much money do you make a year?"

"Can't tell you that."

"Why not? I might want to be an agent if it pays good."

"I make a living."

"Good health insurance? I mean other than that Obama care."

"Yes."

"What's the disadvantage to the job?" Spencer asked.

"Being asked a bunch of questions about the job all the time," the agent told him.

"That would be a drag," Spencer agreed.

***The monsters*** were on the move. There were fourteen creatures roaming the community. Six more shells in the forest around Oak Street were cracking open. As soon as they were out of the shells, they would join the hunt. The agents thought there were two or three to deal with.

There were other urps opening around Elm Street and Ash Street. There were more around the Maple Street cul-de-sac opening. Ted was at the meeting house waiting for the agents to call in with reports of their encounters and kills.

"What is Spencer doing?" Jonathan asked Orlando.

"I think he's talking to the agent."

"Orlando! Come here!" Agent Hawkins called out.

Orlando hurried into the kitchen to see what the agent needed.

"I need to run to the restroom. Keep an eye out and yell if you need me. I'll only be a minute."

"I could have done that," Spencer said.

"Probably because this is my house," Orlando said, trying not to hurt his feelings again. He had to do that a lot.

As soon as the agent closed the door to the bathroom, Orlando saw one of the creatures enter the yard from the woods. Orlando told Jonathan to run to the bathroom and tell the agent it was there.

The creature made a hasty move to the pig. Orlando thought about picking up the flamethrower and going out to face the creature. But as he looked down at it, he knew he had no way of knowing how to fire the thing. What if he caught the house on fire or the woods? The creature had already surrounded the pig before the agent got back, picked up the flamethrower, opened the door, and rushed out.

The creature looked up at him. It smiled. The agent could see blood on the face. An eye erupted toward him and he fired. The agent kept the flames coming as the orange glow of the eye looked at him. Once the creature was dead and gone, so was the pig.

Spencer stepped out of the house with the other two boys following to look at the sight. "Anyone for well-done pork ribs?" Spencer asked. At that moment, three other monsters swarmed into the yard. The three boys ran back into the house. Two of the monsters rushed the agent while one came up from behind.

All three boys yelled for the agent to look behind him, but he couldn't hear since he was flaming the other two. The boys had no way to fight off the third monster. Orlando ran to get the bear spray in the hallway. By the time he got back the agent was dead.

Agent Hawkins had killed the two that had rushed him before the third monster had attacked him. The three boys stood inside the door in shock. Orlando carefully opened the door and checked to make sure the agent was dead. He didn't need to check for a pulse, he could tell by looking at his stomach. He threw up the turkey sandwich and chicken noodles.

Once he was back inside, Spencer asked, "He's dead?"

"Yes."

The agent's radio was sitting on the counter. Orlando picked it up and pushed the button, "Hello, hello."

"Who is this?" a voice came back.

"This is Orlando. Agent Hawkins is dead."

"What happened?" Ted asked.

"He was attacked by four monsters. He killed three of them, but the fourth one got him from behind."

"Are you sure he's dead?"

"Yes."

"All agents. Abort your mission and return to headquarters immediately."

The boys watched as agents came out from behind houses on the street and walked up the street with their weapons drawn. They saw two other agents meet them at the intersection of Maple Street.

Orlando could not believe what they had just witnessed. He collapsed in the recliner and began to cry. He blamed himself for Agent Hawkins' death. He was the one that suggested they get more animals. They got so many that each agent was alone on guard. If Agent Hawkins had had another agent with him, he would still be alive.

*"I should have known better,"* Ted Wilson told the first agent to arrive.

"It's not your fault boss," the agent said.

Ted wanted to pull the agents out of the field, but he knew they still had a job to do. He wasn't sure what to do to keep his agents safe. It finally came to him.

Once all the agents were inside, Ted said, "You're going back out, but only in groups of two. Pick out the best locations and go there. If the animal has already been killed, go to one of the other locations."

"I thought there were only two or three left. How could he have been attacked by four monsters," an agent asked.

"More shells must have opened," he said. "Cover each other's backs."

The agents left again to fight the demon monsters.

Ted was so angry he wanted to climb inside the glass cube and rip the monster apart with his bare hands. This was his biggest blunder since becoming a lead agent. He looked at the monster, and it smiled at him.

He threw a chair at the thing. It bounced off the glass. The creature smiled bigger.

The agents moved out in teams of two. As they separated and went to their assigned spots, they sensed that this night was different than the night before. Each twosome went to the animals they had secured in backyards and each animal they came to was found lifeless in a heap with their stomachs ripped open. The monsters had already struck.

They began reporting back to Ted. He grew angrier with each report. As the two agents who went behind Rufus Langley's house came back around, they were attacked by two of the monsters. They came screaming down the side of the house. The men fired the flamethrowers at the creatures, and they melted into the grass. The wood siding of the house caught on fire. The men rushed to the house to put the fire out.

The fire spread quickly up the side to the roof. One of the agents found the garden hose hooked up to the faucet. He turned it on and tried to put out the fire, but it was no use. The fire was out of control. They radioed Ted and gave him the address. By the time the fire trucks arrived, the house was engulfed.

Two other agents killed one of the monsters as they walked toward the meeting house on Maple Street. Almost every agent told of seeing monsters around every corner. Shots could be heard all around the neighborhood by the residents that night.

The final kill count was one agent, nine monsters, six chickens, three sheep, two goats and two small pigs for the night. The problem was getting worse. Ted now welcomed the help from Washington.

Monday

***Orlando and his two best friends were awake*** at midnight and staring out his bedroom window at the house in flames at the end of Maple Street. They wondered what had caused the fire. Orlando knew no one was living there since Rufus had been killed.

"I bet they caught it on fire with the flamethrower," Spencer said.

"That would be stupid," Jonathan said. The flames rose high in the sky when the firemen arrived. Orlando spotted one of the monsters in his yard.

"Look, there's one of the monsters," Orlando said.

"Is it going to go toward the firemen?" Orlando saw a few men standing around the house. He figured some agents were guarding against the monster's attacks.

The monster started toward the fire and then turned and slinked back toward the woods.

"Is it going to be like this forever?" Jonathan asked, not expecting a real answer.

"I don't know," Orlando said.

"I wish there was something we could do to help," Jonathan said.

"We have helped. We've found the shells. We caught the monster that is in the cube. We've even killed monsters."

"I just feel useless sitting here watching everything that is going on," Jonathan said.

"I know what you mean," Spencer said.

The other two boys looked at him and Jonathan finally took the opening, "You're useless most of the time."

"Hey! That's not very nice," Spence said.

***During the night*** the creatures dropped a total of seventy-nine more urps in the woods and around the community.

# Chapter 21

*The firemen* were able to keep the fire from spreading to the houses nearby and the forest. The house though was burnt to the ground. The three boys stood in front of it and looked at the destruction. The smoke smell was awful.

*Ted's boss, Charles Morton,* arrived at ten that morning. He was met at the airport by two agents. Other agents were set to arrive later in the morning. Charles walked past the glass cube and into Ted's Office, which was no more than a small desk and a couple of chairs.

Ted looked worn out, sleepless, and beside himself.

"You read the report from last night?"

"Yes. How are you doing?"

"Honestly, not very well. I'm at a loss here. The monsters keep coming. We've lost good men here."

"Maybe the vice president's idea wasn't so dumb," Charles said.

"This is a great community. It was peaceful, beautiful and the people are great considering what they are going through. They deserve better."

"We're fighting something we know nothing about. I'm surprised there hasn't been more losses."

"Tell that to the families that have lost loved ones," Ted said.

"I want to see this monster," Charles said.

"It hides during the day under the microwave. You'll see it tonight when he comes out."

"Twenty more agents are arriving today."

"The creatures are growing in numbers. We were fighting two or three. Last night there were ten to twenty. Who knows how many there will be tonight," Ted told him.

Ted took him to the tent. He showed him the shells the creatures come out of. He told how they had searched the area for the shells and destroyed them. Altogether, we and the leaders of the community have destroyed over a hundred shells.

The scientists in the tent told him they had no clue what the creatures were or where they came from.

"You're still thinking extra-terrestrial?" he asked.

"That's the only conclusion we can come up with," one of the scientists said. "Their composition and abilities to grow and shrink in no time is unheard of."

*The three boys* returned to Orlando's house. It was around eight-thirty. Orlando knew his mother would be leaving for work soon.

They walked in and she was in the kitchen eating eggs and toast before work.

"Did you see the fire last night?" Orlando asked.

"What fire?" she asked.

"Rufus Langley's house burnt down."

"How? I thought I smelled smoke this morning."

"From what we could find out, one of the agents was killing a creature with the flamethrower and caught the house on fire."

"What time was that?"

"Around midnight," Jonathan answered.

"I took a shower and went straight to bed. I was tired. I have eight hours at the grocery today and then a house to clean afterward. Won't be home until around dark. Are you okay?"

"Yeah, Mom. I'll be fine. Are there any more eggs?"

"There's plenty. There is bacon in there if you want to fry it."

Francine finished her meal and then headed to work. She felt guilty about leaving Orlando alone so often, but she couldn't afford someone to watch him, and he never got into trouble while she was gone. It had been this way for the past two years. They did what they had to do to get by.

The community had always been safe with good, kind neighbors.

Orlando asked, "Who wants bacon and eggs?"

They all did. Orlando got out a package of bacon and began fried it. Jonathan cracked seven eggs into a bowl.

"What do you want me to do?" Spencer asked.

"Why don't you fix the toast and get out the butter and jam?"

"Okay," Spencer said.

Within a half hour the boys were eating and talking about what to do the rest of the day. Orlando gave Storm a slice of bacon.

"Do you want to go out and search for shells?" Orlando asked. Just as he said that he heard thunder in the distance. Jonathan pulled out his phone and saw that rain was moving into the area for the next few hours.

"I could call August and we could play board games."

"Okay." Spencer didn't say anything at first, but then he said, "Let's call Rhonda Lewis and invite her."

They ignored him.

"Can you beat the rain?" Orlando asked August.

"I've got a rain slicker if I need it. Be there in a few minutes," she said.

Orlando went and opened the garage door so she could pull the bike inside to keep it from getting wet. The rain started before she got there, but not by much. She entered the house and Orlando offered her a towel.

"I thought I was going to beat it," she said, and smiled at Orlando.

They talked about the house burning down as they set up the careers board. Orlando got her something to drink and they started the game.

*Sam McGill went to visit* John Dunbar before the rain started. He sat at the kitchen table drinking coffee as they discussed what was happening.

"I don't know what we can do to help," John told him.

"I'm at a loss too," Sam said.

The two men seemed to have gotten past their feuding in this time of uncertainty.

"It seems like they do the same thing each day and night with the same results."

"And it's getting worse," Sam added.

"The community has lost access to the pool. We only get to use it a few months of the year," John said.

"Have you thought about maybe having pickleball courts built? It's become very popular," Sam told him. "They say it's very popular with the older crowd."

"We could bring it up at a meeting once this monster thing is over."

*While John and Sam talked about pickleball,* another conference call to Washington was taking place.

The head honcho of AARO, Dale Cole, was leading the call.

"I've been going over the updates. We have a situation on our hands," he said. "So far, we've been able to keep it from becoming a nation-wide panic, but that's where I think it's headed. This is worse than Roswell.

"I've been given orders by the President to end this now. I'm calling in the National Guard to help secure and destroy the creatures."

Ted Wilson spoke up, "Sir, that will ensure a nation-wide panic. How do you explain that?"

"Let us worry about that. You guys do not talk to the media. The troops will be arriving by this evening," he hung up.

Charles Morton and Ted Wilson looked at each other, both realizing this wasn't good for their careers.

"He didn't even give me a chance to weigh in or do anything. I mean why send me here?" Charles said. Ted could see that his boss was truly upset. He was upset also. But truth be told, he had no answers on how to get rid of the monsters. They just kept coming.

*With the rising number* of creatures last night came more urps dropped in the community and the woods. By the evening there would be over a hundred monsters on the loose hunting for liver. Rain was falling hard across Minnesota. The kids thought the thunder sounded like it was right on top of them. Lightning struck all around them. They had the window shades open on the patio doors so they could watch the rain fall.

"I'm going into sports," Spencer announced. He moved his token into the sports section and landed on a square that paid him ten thousand dollars.

"Ha, ha, ha," he laughed.

"It's the only way you'll ever make any money in sports," Jonathan told him.

A lightning bolt struck a tree somewhere in the woods behind the house. They could hear the crack of the wood splitting. All four of the kids jumped in their seats.

*The monsters had never* had rain dropped on them. They didn't mind the water at all. In fact, they welcomed it.

*Francine called home* during her break to make sure everything was okay.

"We're fine," Orlando told her.

"We just heard on the radio that the National Guard had been called in to help the agents," she told him.

"Wow!"

"They're taking it more seriously now," she told him.

"Maybe all the monsters will drown in this rain," Orlando offered.

"That would be good. There are a couple of frozen pizzas in the freezer. What are you doing?"

"The guys are still here. August came and we're playing board games right now. Later, we're all going to get drunk and party!"

She laughed and said, "Save some for me. Love you."

"Love you too, Mom."

Orlando hung up and asked, "Anyone for pizza?"

"Yeah!" Spencer yelled.

Orlando went to the freezer and found the Detroit style pepperoni and sausage pizza and turned on the oven to preheat.

"Your turn, scumhead," Spencer said.

"Just for that, no pizza for you!"

"No soup for you!" Jonathan cried out. They all laughed.

*Lucas West* couldn't concentrate on his work. His mind kept going back to the kiss. He hadn't enjoyed the company of a woman since his divorce until he met Francine. He had dated a few times. But usually, it was only one date. He found most of the ladies boring or full of themselves.

Francine was different. She was down to earth. She was attractive, but not overly done up. She was funny and fun to be with. She worked hard and loved her son. What was not to like?

Lucas had been married for eight years. He had met his wife, Sharon, when they were in college at the University of Minnesota. She was studying design. They hit it off and married after graduation. They had decided not to have children until their careers were cemented and they were settled.

Five years later, she told Lucas that she didn't want children. This was a total surprise to Lucas, who had always wanted kids. They argued about this change of heart on her part. The next few years were filled with more disagreements and sad episodes for both.

They finally concluded that they couldn't go on like they had been. Neither of them was happy. They divorced and went their separate ways.

He was now thirty-eight. Francine had told him she was thirty-five.

*The four kids* spent the afternoon playing different games, listening to The Beatles, and watching the rain come down. The forecast called for it to rain the rest of the day and night.

After four o'clock that afternoon, August's mother called her and told her to be home around five for dinner.

"Could I invite Orlando? His mother is working late."

"I guess so," her mother said.

Around four-thirty they all left Orlando's house and headed home. Orlando put on a poncho and rode his bike alongside August to her house. They parked the bikes under the front porch of her house. Orlando took off his poncho and followed August into the house.

August's mother came in to greet Orlando. "Thank you for having me," Orlando told her.

"We're glad you could come," she said. "Will this rain ever stop?"

"Probably," Orlando said.

"Someday, Mom," August said.

Orlando always appreciated being invited for dinner by his friends. But this was different. He had never had a girlfriend before. He knew he needed to be respectful and courteous during the meal. He didn't want her parents to think she had made a bad decision in choosing a boyfriend. But perhaps they thought he was just a friend.

During the meal, the talk turned to the monsters. Her father said that he had heard the National Guard had been called in to help.

"My mom said she heard the same thing," Orlando said. "We haven't seen any of them yet."

"Well, something has to be done," August's mother said.

"We're fortunate that more people haven't been killed," her father said.

"And that they haven't spread to other areas," Orlando added.

"That would be awful," her mother said.

The meal was good, and Orlando thanked them for the invitation. After eating, there was a break in the rain. It had slowed down.

"I think I should head home before it storms again," Orlando told the family.

"Come back anytime. It was a pleasure having you," Mrs. Simms said.

He and August walked out onto the porch, and she quickly gave him a kiss before he took off. When he got to Maple Street he saw a caravan of sand-colored trucks near the meeting house. The National Guard had arrived. They were jumping out of the back of the trucks. He stopped at the intersection and watched them. He then decided to get a closer look.

He saw John Dunbar standing in front of the meeting house observing the swarm of soldiers arriving. He rode his bike over to him.

"There are a lot of them," Orlando said.

"It looks like we're being invaded," John said.

"Do you know what the plans are for tonight?" Orlando asked him.

"They haven't told me anything. It looks like they have enough manpower to put five men at every house."

Orlando knew there were fifty-five homes in the subdivision. He had asked once. He doubted John's math was right about the number of Guardsmen, but figured he was exaggerating.

It was getting late, and Orlando decided to head home. The rain was starting to come down harder again. He needed to let Storm out before it got dark. He knew it would get dark earlier due to the cloud cover. It already looked like twilight time, and it was only seven-thirty.

**Ted Wilson, Charles Morton** and the leader of the National Guard, Chase Banks, worked together on assignments for the night. No animals were bought to tie up. They figured they had enough men to cover the entire neighborhood. They were going to send the men out in groups of three and place them between every other house. The men had never used flamethrowers before and had to be given a quick lesson on them. They weren't that difficult to learn.

They were also armed with their usual M16 or XM7 assault rifles and a M17 pistol on their hip. They wore rain gear which made it a little clumsier with all the weapons they were carrying.

Outside the perimeter of the community were news crews eager to get information on what was going on. Ted Wilson made his way over to them and made a statement.

"Once it gets dark, it is not safe to be outside. You'll need to be inside your vehicles or leave."

"Why? Are there really monsters roaming the streets of The Woods at night?" a reporter asked.

Ted had to tell them about the dangers. He didn't want more blood on his hands.

"Yes. Believe me when I tell you that you need to get off the streets before dark."

He turned and left as a hundred questions were being fired at him. He knew some of the reporters would risk their lives to get the story. He had warned them and would probably be reprimanded for it.

*As Orlando rode home on his bike,* he could feel something in the air that he had never felt before. It felt like an electric charge. He didn't know if it was from expectations of not knowing what was going to happen or if there really was something in the air.

He had just turned onto Oak Street when his mother rode up beside him. She honked and waved.

He asked her, "What are you doing home?"

"Something told me I needed to be home this evening. Did you see the National Guard?"

"I was just up there."

"Lucas is coming over to stay with us this evening."

"Okay. I need to let Storm out before it gets dark." He took Storm out the back door. He wondered why his mother would invite Lucas over. His phone rang. He looked at the screen and saw that it was Jonathan.

"What?" he answered.

"Something is happening. I can feel it."

"Me too."

Orlando looked up the street and saw the Guardsmen filing down the road. Smaller groups peeled off at each street.

"I gotta go. Call me later." He ended the call and stood there while Storm watered a bush. Three Guardsmen approached him and one of them said, "You'd better get inside."

"I know that. Just letting Storm finish up."

"A fine-looking pup," he said.

"Good luck tonight."

"Yeah. You got monsters, huh?"

"You'll see," I said, and took Storm back inside. I didn't like the way the Guardsman grinned when he mentioned monsters – like he didn't believe a word of it.

"Just as he closed the door, Orlando saw Lucas pull into the driveway."

The Guardsman said something to him when he got out of the car. Lucas nodded and started for the door. Orlando had it open before Lucas could ring the doorbell.

"Good evening," Lucas said as he came into the house.

"Hi. Mom is changing. She'll be out soon."

"There is something strange about this evening," Lucas said

"You mean besides the monsters thing?"

He nodded.

"Yeah. I can sense it to."

Francine walked into the room looking like she had fixed herself up. Lucas kissed her cheek in greeting. Orlando noticed his mother's smile.

"This is crazy, isn't it?" she said.

"The Guardsmen are all over the neighborhood," Lucas told her.

The three of them stood at the bay window and watched as it got darker. The rain continued coming down hard.

# Chapter 22

***In Washington,*** the president walked into the War Room. There were many others seated around the table including senators, generals, advisers and the representatives from Minnesota. Everyone stood as he made his way to the head of the table. They all sat when he sat.

Large TVs covered the walls of the room. On the TV's were surveillance feeds of the The Woods neighborhood. Each Guardsman and agent had been fitted with infrared bodycams that filmed everything they saw and transmitted back to the TVs on the walls.

"Gentlemen, what is happening now?" the president asked.

The National Guard representative answered, "Mr. President, we have groups of three spread throughout the community ready to eliminate the creatures when they come out from hiding. We have the area on complete lockdown."

"What are the chances that these creatures have spread to other regions?" the president asked.

"There have been no sightings or reports of that happening. But we can't be sure. There are no other communities within five miles. There are a few farms, but with no activity."

"Good."

***Orlando, Francine and Lucas*** stood watching the men outside as the darkness came. Jonathan stood at the window with his parents at their own house. Spencer was hunkered down deep in his bed, the rain hitting hard against his window.

Mrs. Ruth Johnson was watching TV, completely oblivious to what was going on. Both cats were sitting on her lap.

Sam McGill and Patsy were watching the men between their house and the Nelson's. John Dunbar was inside the meeting house with Ted Wilson, Charles Morton and Chase Banks. They waited with great anticipation.

The community's hopes rode with what would happen that night. There had been too many residents and pets killed. Folks wanted to enjoy the summer like they had in the past. They wanted to go for walks after the sun set. They wanted to walk the trails in the woods again without being scared. They wanted their normal lives back again.

Without warning, a shot was fired from somewhere in the community. Lucas thought it sounded like it had come from Elm Street. Another shot was heard down the block. Then they heard shots coming from all around. They watched as the three men in the yard ran between the houses. They saw what they thought was light from the flamethrower.

They heard a man scream. Orlando thought it sounded more like the screams of the creatures. He had heard it many times.

***In the Presidential War Room,*** the men watched in horror as they saw the footage of the monsters attacking the men. There were so many of them. On each TV the Guardsmen were surrounded by monsters.

Suddenly, in a flash, a purple haze filled the sky, and each screen went blank.

"What happened?!" the president shouted.

***Orlando couldn't believe what he was seeing.*** One moment the Guardsmen were fighting monsters, the rain was pouring down on them, and gunshots were heard across The Woods, but then, in an instant the rain stopped, the gunfire stopped, the sky and air turned a light purple and the creatures who were in the front yard began to slowly rise into the sky. When the sky turned purple, everyone's overwhelming fear turned into a calm curiosity as if the haze had psychologic medicinal properties.

Orlando opened the front door and stepped out into the yard. His mom and Lucas followed him. They stood and watched the monsters rise like white light beams into the purple sky. Folks across the community left their houses to watch the spectacle unfold.

Spencer saw the purple haze outside his window, got up, and ran to look out his window.

The monsters looked like they were stretched upward while still touching the ground until they parted with the earth and shot like bullets into the sky. Unopened shells rose like meteors toward a large round object high in the sky, leaving a trail of light behind them as they flew.

The men from the meeting house stood outside watching the strange phenomenon. The creature in the glass cube was screaming bloody murder wanting to join the others in the resurrection. It climbed to the ceiling of the cube to be closer to its mother ship. It cried out a mournful sound.

Orlando thought it looked like hundreds of monsters and shells shot into the sky. It was. He looked across the street and saw Jonathan looking into the sky.

Mrs. Johnson's TV was shut off and she couldn't get it back on. She then noticed the purple haze outside her window.

Orlando pulled his phone from his pocket but couldn't turn it on.

The ship had blocked everything, even the rain, to accomplish its mission.

Almost magically, the purple haze disappeared, and the airship disappeared behind the clouds and the rain began to fall again. The Guardsmen came out from around the house. They looked shaken.

One of the men said, “Craziest thing I’ve ever seen.”

Orlando told him, “Just a normal day for us.”

Orlando lifted his arms to the sky and let the rain fall on his face and he danced. Lucas took Francine in his arms and kissed her, and they began twirling around in the rain.

# Chapter 23

Tuesday

**The reporters** that were stationed outside the subdivision had a good story, but due to the strange circumstances, they had no video footage or photographs to accompany their fantastic reports of the incident.

**The president** wanted to hold someone responsible for losing the feed to the event. He was informed of what happened, but he was extremely disappointed in not seeing it for himself. But there was no one to blame except those on the spaceship.

**The next day Orlando** invited Jonathan, Spencer, August and April to his house. They spent the day talking about the night before and jumping and dancing to Jimi Hendrix's song *Purple Haze.*

He directed Alexa to play the song on repeat. Orlando couldn't remember a day that he had been happier.

Three days later

**The pool opened** again on Friday. The tent was gone. The meeting house sat empty again. The cube and creature had been moved to somewhere in Virginia. Children were playing again in the playground. People were taking walks in the woods with their bear spray. The bears and moose didn't seem so scary anymore.

The community was back to normal except for the residents that had been killed by the creatures. They had a memorial in the meeting house to remember those they had lost.

December

**Snow blanketed** the community. Christmas lights hung from every house in the neighborhood. A large fir tree stood at the entrance of The Woods. It had been decorated, and the community residents came out for the lighting ceremony on the first Saturday of December. They sung *Silent Night.*

Orlando had been out shoveling driveways and sidewalks to make money to help his mom and to buy Christmas gifts for his family and friends.

He invited August to his house two nights before Christmas to watch the movie, *Elf.* It was Orlando's favorite Christmas movie. Francine made hot chocolate and Christmas cookies and invited Lucas. A nice fire in the fireplace made the room warm and cozy. A bowl of uncracked mixed nuts sat on the coffee table in front of them. The bowl of nuts was a family tradition, although they seldom got cracked opened and eaten.

In the middle of the movie something caught Orlando and August's eye.

"Did I just see one of those nuts move?" August asked.

Orlando got up, picked up the bowl and threw the nuts into the fireplace. "No way am I taking a chance." They looked at him and then laughed. The two couples snuggled together as they watched the movie.

May

**Lucas and Francine** were married in a small community church they had begun attending.

Orlando was best man.

Storm was the ringbearer.

Francine was expecting a month later.

*The End*

Dear Readers,

Thank you again for your support and readership. It means so much to me.

I realize this novel is a journey into another realm. Let me explain, I had a dream one night and when I woke up, I remembered every detail of it as if it had actually happened to me. That seldom happens, if ever. I took it as a sign and began writing it down that day. It turned into this novel. The beginning of this book was that dream.

The final novel in the Kentucky Summers 2 series is being written and will be out before you know it, as they say.

I hope you enjoyed this book. It is meant to be fun and put a little scary into your life. Most of us enjoy that.

I need to thank my editors, Cārucandra Klupp and Terry Cornett.

I also want to thank my card playing friend, Jim Culler, for the photography and design of the picture on the cover.

Cārucandra Klupp designed the book again. You have been such a blessing in my life. What would I do without you?

Terry Cornett kept encouraging me with this book, asking for more pages as I wrote. She is a godsend.

Mostly I thank God for his many mercies and help.

Keep reading and imagining.

Blessings,

Tim Callahan www.timcallahan.net
Email – timcal21@yahoo.com

The **All-domain Anomaly Resolution Office (AARO)** is an office within the United States Office of the Secretary of Defense that investigates unidentified flying objects (UFOs) and other phenomena in the air, sea, and/or space and/or on land: sometimes referred to as "unidentified aerial phenomena" or "unidentified anomalous phenomena" (UAP).